KIDNAPPED!

Many men blocked Squanto's way to the water. They grabbed him. He cried out, "Nakooma!"

More arrows rattled onto the wooden deck. And then a noise like all the thunder in the sky exploded from one of the big black tubes. A puff of smoke burst before his peoples' canoes and scattered them on the water.

The great canoe quickly outdistanced the Pawtuxets. The last thing Squanto heard was Nakooma crying his name . . .

SQUANTO

A WARRIOR'S TALE

SQUANTO

A WARRIOR'S TALE

A novel by Ron Fontes and Justine Korman
Based on the motion picture from
Walt Disney Pictures
Executive Producer Don Carmody
Based on the screenplay written by
Darlene Craviotto
Produced by Kathryn F. Galan
Directed by Xavier Koller

Troll Associates

Library of Congress Cataloging-in-Publication Data

Fontes, Ron.
    Walt Disney Pictures presents Squanto A Warrior's Tale: a novel by Ron
Fontes and Justine Korman; based on the screenplay written by Darlene
Craviotto.
        p.   cm.
    Summary: Squanto is kidnapped to England and put on display, until
he escapes and is aided in his return to America by friendly monks.
    ISBN 0-8167-2502-0 (pbk.)
    1. Squanto—Juvenile fiction.   2. Wampanoag Indians—Juvenile
fiction.   [1. Squanto—Fiction.   2. Wampanoag Indians—Fiction.
3. Indians of North America—Fiction.   4. Pilgrims (New Plymouth
Colony)—Fiction.]   I. Korman, Justine.   II. Craviotto, Darlene.
III. Walt Disney Pictures.   IV. Title.   V. Title: Squanto A Warrior's
Tale.
PZ7.F73577Wal   1994
[Fic]—dc20   93-48122

Special thanks to Virginia King and Hunter Heller.
Photos by Attila Dory.

Printed in the United States of America.
10 9 8 7 6 5 4 3 2 1

CHAPTER

1

▽△▽△▽△▽△▽

This is how the story begins.

A young warrior arranged a circle of stones on the beach. He purified the air with handfuls of burning sweet grass. He sat in the circle of stones and opened his heart to Kissuulk the creator. The warrior's name was Squanto. He was the son of Mooshawset, a *sachem,* or chief, of the Pawtuxet tribe.

Above Squanto, a hawk cried out as it swooped in the fresh winds blowing off the murmuring sea. Sea gulls wheeled and dipped over the waves. The rising sun warmed the young man's lean, healthy body. The world was in balance and he was in balance with the world.

***

An explosion of shouts and rattling sticks shattered the silence of the forest. With loincloths flapping and scalp locks streaming behind them, Pawtuxet warriors leaped from the leafy treetops to rush the deer feeding in the clearing. The terrified deer swung around and sprang for the protection of the deep woods. Their white tails flashed and bobbed across the open meadow.

But the unfortunate animals soon found themselves herded between two rows of wooden stakes that narrowed like a funnel. They were trapped!

The warriors raised their bows and arrows. Their dark eyes focused on their leader, Mooshawset. Beside him stood his son, Squanto, an arrow already in his bow. He was impatient for the kill.

At Mooshawset's signal, the bows sang and the air hummed with whizzing arrows. Squanto's arrow found its mark. A smile flickered across his handsome face. His nimble fingers quickly drew another arrow from his birch-bark quiver.

Doomed deer fell under the fatal rain. But one great stag leaped over the stakes to freedom. Squanto gasped with excitement. Here was an animal worthy of a warrior! He and Mooshawset chased the great creature deeper into the forest bright with autumn leaves.

Dense branches and gnarled roots could not stop Squanto. He hurdled rocks and ducked limbs as he dashed through the dappled light. White birch trunks streaked past his vision.

Sensing the stag's goal, Mooshawset split off from his son. He found the great red deer at the edge of a cliff with nowhere to run. Thundering waterfalls below the jagged rocks swallowed the hard breathing of man and beast.

The stag faced his enemy and lowered his heavy rack of sharp antlers. Mooshawset aimed his mighty bow. But at that moment, the wise sachem looked into the trapped, but fearless, beast's eyes. He saw they shared the deep secrets of nature. They were one in spirit. Mooshawset lowered his bow. Just then, Squanto rushed to the cliff and aimed his own arrow at the cornered stag.

"No, my son," Mooshawset said quietly.

"But I've beaten him, Father!" Squanto protested. His young heart beat fast with the glory of the hunt.

Mooshawset said, "There is a time to kill and a time not to kill. Put your weapon down. We have killed enough for today."

Squanto's defiance faded, giving way to the deep respect he had for his wise father. The stag dashed away with a clatter of hooves.

* * *

Children shouted joyful greetings as the swift canoes of Squanto and the warriors beached on the sandy shore. Gulls shrieked as they circled the low-sided, birch-bark canoes laden with fresh deer meat and hides. There was even more activity in the Pawtuxet village.

In the fields near their small village, women and girls were harvesting corn. Some hoed the weeds from pumpkin patches and rows of beans. The leaves were turning and already winter was in the air. To be ready for the coming snows, the people of the village would dry the beans and squash, smoke meat, and make cakes of nuts and berries.

Amid the domed birch-bark wigwams and the long house, people ground corn and tanned hides. An old woman was weaving on a finger loom. A young boy carried a heavy basket of clamshells to the old man carving *wampum* beads. Some men and women were making a new birch-bark canoe.

The women used deer sinews to stitch the sheets of bark to the bent, wooden frame. But it was the return of Squanto and the warriors that attracted the children that day.

As soon as Squanto stepped from his canoe, the children gathered around him. He played the game of "Stones and Bones," hiding pebbles and small bones in his hands and hiding his hands behind his back. The laughing children tried to guess which hand the stones were in. When Squanto had them all giggling, he scattered the bones on the sand for the children to gather.

Squanto smiled at a graceful young woman working in the cornfield. She turned to look at him, a basket of corn balanced against her hip. Her long, unbraided hair hung like a glossy curtain around her lovely face. She was not the only young woman in their tribe, but none were as beautiful as Nakooma. Squanto smiled because they would be married the next day.

"Was it good hunting, Squanto?" Nakooma asked.

Squanto thrilled to hear her speak his name. "The hunting was not as good as the return," he said.

* * *

"O Great Kissuulk, Creator of Earth and Sun, we gather for the marriage of Nakooma of the Hawk Clan and Squanto of the Wolf Clan." The medicine man, or *shaman*, in his black deerskins chanted before a fire burning in the center of the long house. Dressed in their finest beaded, painted clothes, Nakooma and her family stood on one side of the crackling flames. Squanto and his parents were on the other.

One by one, each member of Nakooma's family stepped away from the fire. Her mother, Nosapocket, was the last to leave. Nosapocket kissed her daughter's cheek and whispered, "Be faithful and honest always, Nakooma."

Then she left her daughter alone by the fire.

Mooshawset held up a shiny, fringed *wampung* belt made of purple and white beads fashioned from clamshells. The history of the Pawtuxet tribe was woven into its patterns: victories and defeats, rich harvests and famine, and all the tales of their people.

To Squanto, Mooshawset said, "Someday you will be a sachem. You will wear the wampung belt. You will carry on the history of our tribe."

Mooshawset was a sachem, the chief

among the Pawtuxet. He was not a king and did not rule by birth. He ruled because the people found him to be fair and wise. Mooshawset hoped that someday Squanto would temper his courage with wisdom. And perhaps Squanto, too, would become a sachem. But that was something the young man would have to earn for himself.

Squanto leaned down to kiss the belt. Then Mooshawset and his wife stepped away from their son, leaving Squanto alone on his side of the fire.

Slowly, bride and groom turned to face each other. Squanto reached out in the bright light and gently placed Nakooma's braids over her shoulder, so all could see that Nakooma was now his wife. She took his hand and they were joined as one.

The people danced and feasted on deer meat, baked clams, sweet squash, and a savory succotash of fish, corn, and beans. Nakooma took a hawk feather from her painted deerskin dress.

"With my love, I honor your spirit — the spirit of the Hawk. With his feather, I honor you," she said. With her dark eyes sparkling, she lovingly slipped the feather into Squanto's long hair. "His protection is forever."

"I will always keep it close," Squanto promised.

* * *

The next morning, Squanto and Nakooma stood before the shaman, eager to receive one last blessing. Squanto carried a bundle of arrows and spears. Nakooma carried a backpack that was heavy with parched corn, smoked meat, snowshoes, blankets, and other supplies.

The shaman said, "Today you begin your spiritual journey."

Mooshawset addressed his son and new daughter-in-law. "You will stay in the forest to learn from each other, to learn what nature will teach you. You must not return until the next harvest."

The newlyweds nodded obediently. Everyone in the tribe watched as they left the village, not to return for a year.

Yet they had not gone far across the meadow when Squanto saw something very strange. A great, black canoe — bigger than a long house, as big as a whale — glided across the bay. His warrior's senses tingled with danger. What tribe could this be? He knew the canoes of all their neighbors: the Nausetts, Pocomtuc, Mahicans, and Wampanoag. Sometimes they came in peace and sometimes they came for war. But never did they build a canoe such as this.

"We must go back, Nakooma," Squanto said, determined to protect his tribe.

Nakooma felt the danger too, but said, "We will be breaking our vows."

Squanto took his vows seriously, but he was even more concerned with protecting his people. He took Nakooma by the hand and they returned to the village.

CHAPTER

2

▼△▼△▼△▼△▼

A smaller canoe left the wooden "whale" and approached the shore. Strange men with outlandish clothes and faces as white as spirits paddled the oddly shaped canoe.

Pawtuxet warriors seized their weapons. Squanto clutched a spear, but his father stepped before him and said gravely, "You must go with your bride."

Squanto's jaw set defiantly. "My bride will wait until we know our village is safe." So saying, Squanto and the warriors walked to the water where the pale men were beaching their canoe.

Their faces were hairy, like animals, and some wore tall headdresses with plumes.

The newcomers' clothes hung loosely about them in great, baggy folds of fabulous color and design. Even at a distance, Squanto could see these clothes were not made of deerskin or any other animal hide. Their bright colors were like the plumage of birds.

One man wore the color of freshly spilled blood and carried a long, shiny rod. *Was this a weapon?* Squanto wondered. The man's chest was encased in a gleaming shell, like a lobster. He wore a gleaming shell on his head too.

A meek man, more drably dressed than the others, stepped forward and spoke in Algonquin. "Greetings! We come in peace."

Another man held out what looked like a gleaming squash. When Mooshawset shook the thing, it made a sound unlike any Squanto had ever heard. CLANG!

In addition to the bell, the strangers had brought with them a great box. They spilled its contents on the ground: metal pots and knives; combs and bracelets; bright cloth, like the fabric they wore, woven so tightly you could barely see the strands; and beads much finer than wampum, pierced with tiny holes and in every color of the rainbow. And things that were like clamshells, only you could see your face in them, like a still pond.

The villagers gathered around as the little

man spoke. "These come from our land across the water. We will trade them for things from your land." He gestured to the beaver pelts and baskets of fruit piled outside the wigwams.

The women examined the strange stuff from the box, laughing and giggling at the oddness of it. One of the hairy men looked long and greedily at Nakooma, as if he wanted to put her in a box and keep her. Squanto stepped between them and glared, until the man looked away nervously.

The tribe was most interested in the strangers' weapons and insisted on a demonstration. A pumpkin was placed on a tree stump. The lobster man in the blood-red coat aimed a small tube at the fruit. The tube made a great noise, which startled the tribe. But the pumpkin remained unharmed, and everyone laughed.

Then Squanto easily placed an arrow in the center of the pumpkin. THUNK!

The lobster man's face was almost as red as his coat. He seized a long tube from one of his hard-shelled warriors. This tube thundered even louder, and the pumpkin exploded.

The warriors were amazed. They could kill many deer with such a tube.

At words from their leader, the little man

spoke again. "We need five strong warriors to carry the furs to the ship."

Squanto thought the little man did not like saying those words. But when Mooshawset nodded, Squanto was first to volunteer. If there was danger, he wanted to be there! He helped his fellow warriors, Pocknet and Attaquin, load beaver pelts into canoes as the strangers paddled ahead in their oddly shaped craft.

Nakooma asked her husband, "Do you trust them?"

He did not, but Squanto replied, "My friends have the courage to go. I must go with them."

Squanto was not afraid, but Nakooma was. Her husband was so brave that he did not always stop to think before he acted. He was not old enough to be as wise as his father. He could not imagine a bear that could beat him or a warrior who might trick him in battle. Squanto had always been the best young warrior in their tribe.

"We're breaking the commitment," Nakooma said, hoping to change his mind.

"When I'm back, we will continue our bridal journey," Squanto assured her. "Don't be worried."

She felt a little better, but was still troubled when Squanto jumped into the canoe and pushed off.

The great canoe looked even stranger as Squanto drew close. Black tubes jutted over its high, carved sides. The mask of a woman stared from the prow. Many ropes, like the web of a spider, swung from the long, skinny, bare trees poking from its back.

Squanto helped Pocknet and Attaquin carry the heavy beaver pelts up a rope ladder on the side of the great canoe. The other two warriors stayed in the canoes to steady them. Sea gulls cried above.

A man shouted and suddenly the rope webs lifted huge sheets, white as birch bark, that puffed out like big bellies full of wind. More ropes hauled the strangers' small canoe from the water. Squanto saw so many new things, he could not begin to guess what purpose they served. What a tale this would be for Nakooma and the tribe! Someday this story would make a great pattern in the wampung belt.

Some of the pale men led Squanto and his companions down into the dark belly of the great canoe. The air reeked of sweat and rot. A rat squeaked on the sagging steps.

Squanto nearly lost his footing when the great canoe lurched. He looked around, but the strange men pushed him to make him go deeper. And then the canoe lurched again.

Squanto suddenly noticed a Nausett

warrior tied up in a dank room full of wooden baskets. SLAM! Suddenly the sun was gone, all but a few dusty streaks. The Pawtuxets cried out, and the pale men grabbed them and tried to put knives to their throats.

Squanto fought with all his strength and battled his way back up the ladder, but he was pulled back down. Pocknet and Attaquin freed themselves and scrambled up the ladder.

Furious as a cornered bear, Squanto hurled the pale men into the heap of wooden baskets and followed his friends. The warriors burst through the big, wooden flap and heard the war cry of their tribe rise up from the shore. Squanto heard Nakooma shriek his name above all the other cries.

A shiny stick spoke with thunder. Trying to escape, Pocknet and Attaquin dove overboard into the waters. Squanto saw his father and the warriors of his tribe paddling their canoes, with Nakooma among them. Arrows rained down on the great canoe. At their leader's command, the strangers' long sticks spit fire and clouds of bitter smoke.

Many men blocked Squanto's way to the water. They grabbed him. He cried out, "Nakooma!"

More arrows rattled onto the wooden

deck. And then a noise like all the thunder in the sky exploded from one of the big black tubes. A puff of smoke burst like the pumpkin before his peoples' canoes and scattered them on the water.

The great canoe quickly outdistanced the Pawtuxets. The last thing Squanto heard was Nakooma crying his name.

CHAPTER

3

▼▲▼▲▼▲▼▲▼

"Treat these savages as friends, Mr. Dermer, and you'll find an arrow in your back," said Stephen Harding, the very model of a British officer: stern, duty-bound, hard, and cold. He ignored the swaying lantern over his head and the pitching, groaning ship that lifted and dropped everything in the cabin.

"Steal from them, Mr. Harding," countered Thomas Dermer, "and you'll kill any opportunity to trade with them in the future."

Harding smirked.

"We're following orders, Mr. Dermer. Orders that come from Sir George, who owns this ship and pays our wages," said the ship's captain, Clarence Hunt, a narrow-minded, smug man. Captain Hunt shared Harding's contempt for this soft scholar, who obviously knew his way around a book better than he did an Indian. But they needed Mr. Dermer because only he could speak the savages' tongue.

The three men ate a meager dinner of hardtack and salt pork in the captain's quarters. They were one week out from Cape Cod, Massachusetts, where they had seized the beaver pelts and warriors now locked in the ship's dark hold. The ship, called the *Archangel,* was bound for the England of King James I.

"You've deceived these people and betrayed them," Dermer said.

The other two men just glared at him. Hunt replied, "You've told me, Mr. Dermer, that you hope to be the master of a ship like this one day."

"That is my ambition, yes," said Dermer.

"A dim ambition indeed, if you disappoint Sir George with your disobedience," Hunt sneered.

An officer entered and placed a plate of biscuits on the table. "They still refuse to eat," he reported.

"And they won't eat, as long as they're

locked up like animals," said Dermer. "Allow me to untie them."

"And then they'll eat?" Harding asked. "But what will they eat, Mr. Dermer, hmm? They might begin with you!" Harding pointed a knife at his mild-mannered companion, and the others roared with laughter.

* * *

Down in the hold, Squanto could not hear the laughter. He had just smashed a wooden basket and was trying to cut his ropes on the sharp pieces. He was getting accustomed to being at sea. His cramped muscles strained at the task of keeping the rope taut over the cutting edge. Salty water sloshed around his ankles. Squanto felt the great canoe heave with each breath of the big water.

The Nausett man finally spoke. "Perhaps you will escape the white man and his guns, but you will not escape the water."

"Then let me drown!" Squanto replied. "They will not keep me here!" In his anger, Squanto finally broke the rope binding his hands.

"Very clever, for a Pawtuxet," the warrior remarked.

Squanto just smiled, then crawled across the dirty floor to untie the warrior's hands.

"I am the sachem, Epenow," the Nausett said.

"And I am Squanto."

At a sudden sound above, Epenow put a hand on Squanto's shoulder and whispered, "Patience, nephew."

The warriors returned to their former places, pretending that their hands were still bound behind their backs.

Thomas Dermer came down the steps into the *Archangel's* stinking hold. He carried a bowl of biscuits and was escorted by two rough sailors.

Dermer carefully set down the bowl, then squatted and spoke gently in Algonquin. "My name is Thomas," he began. "I do not ask you to trust me, but I trust you." Despite his fear, Dermer reached behind Squanto to untie his hands. When he saw there were no ropes, he was surprised and moved carefully away. But he gave no sign to the sailors.

"Well, then, eat," Dermer said calmly, and pointed to the food.

Squanto lifted the plate of biscuits, and Dermer smiled. Then Squanto angrily hurled the plate against the wall. The biscuits bounced and scattered. Dermer scrambled away as Squanto attacked. Epenow grabbed the young warrior, while Dermer held the sailors at bay.

Dermer and the sailors backed up the stairs. He looked down at Squanto. Dermer's thoughtful face showed not only fear, but admiration.

"He was mine to kill," Squanto said.

"In time, brother," Epenow said calmly. His wise caution reminded Squanto of his father.

Epenow picked up a biscuit. "They will pay for what they've done to us." He broke the biscuit in half and offered a portion to Squanto.

* * *

Three long, dark, seasick months later, the great canoe slowed to a stop. The waves rocked gently in small swells. Squanto realized they had reached land.

Squanto heard a loud voice he had not heard before. Many small dogs barked. The pale men were very excited.

On the deck of the *Archangel*, Harding and Hunt supervised the unloading of cargo. They had docked in Plymouth, England. Hunt bowed as the ship's owner stepped on board. "Good day, Sir George."

"Mr. Hunt, Mr. Harding, returned alive and well. Good, good. This is a great day for England!" Sir George exclaimed, stroking his large gold ring. "A great day for enterprise, for civilization, for the Plymouth Shipping Company. What a glorious morning it is!" Sir George gushed as he inspected the pelts and other goods.

Eager to please his employer, Harding said, "We've had a very successful voyage, Sir."

"I expect nothing less from you gentlemen," Sir George replied. But his thick lips formed a childish pout. "Tell me, is this the extent of our venture?"

Harding smiled. "Prepare to be astounded, Sir George!"

A cargo hatch creaked open, and Squanto and Epenow, blinking in the sudden sunlight, were dragged from the dark hold. Their cramped legs wobbled beneath them.

Squanto forgot his weakness when he saw the amazing man who strutted the deck before him. During the long voyage, Squanto had grown accustomed to the odd clothing and manner of the pale, hairy-faced men. But this new person looked part human, part pumpkin. He was surrounded by flat-nosed, short-legged stocky creatures that barked like dogs, yet resembled none Squanto had ever seen.

Sir George's pack of nasty bulldogs yapped around his elegant, high-heeled shoes. Embroidered hose covered his chubby legs up to the cuffs of his puffed and slashed brocade breeches. His expansive belly was encased in a pointed doublet of rich velvet, trimmed at every turn with ribbon and lace. His face was framed by a stiff, lace collar. A tall, plumed hat topped his flowing curls.

"My God, look at them!" Sir George said fearfully. He stared in wonder at the half-starved warriors — bare-chested men with tattoos, shell necklaces, and long hair, both dressed in animal-hide leggings and fringed loincloths. The younger one had a feather stuck in his hair. "They're awful! They're horrible! They're wonderful! Mr. Harding, what will happen if I approach them?"

"My men will protect you, Sir," Harding assured the nervous merchant.

The sailors rudely pushed Squanto and Epenow closer to the dandy. The warriors stared in confusion at bustling Plymouth Harbor. The masts were like a winter forest. Fishermen shouted. Sea gulls dipped and screamed in the sky.

"Look, they're frightened," Sir George observed. And their fear gave him courage.

"They've never seen a place like this before," Harding explained.

Sir George approached the warriors. "And never seen the likes of me before, have you?" he demanded. "I am Sir George . . ."

He paused and peered at the brown grease streaking Squanto's arm. He pulled a handkerchief from his sleeve and dabbed at one of the smears. "Good lord, what is that?"

"Bear fat," Dermer answered. "It keeps the bugs away."

"Goodness gracious, how amusing. Disgusting, really. See here, he's wearing it on his face!" Sir George dabbed the handkerchief on Squanto's face. Squanto bit the chubby hand that wore the huge gold ring.

Sir George screamed and pranced around in pain like a toddler stung by a bee. He scuttled away in terror. His dogs barked and growled and snapped their heavy jaws. In the confusion, Squanto wriggled from the sailors' grip. He scuffled with the sailors as they struggled to regain their captive.

Once Squanto was firmly held between several strong sailors, Sir George said, "Mr. Dermer, can these savages understand you?"

"I speak their language, yes," said Dermer.

"Tell them who I am," Sir George commanded. "Tell them I run the Plymouth Shipping Company. This is my ship, and I own them!"

Mr. Dermer shook his head. "They will never understand it, Sir, that one man can own another."

"Then we'll make them understand it!" Sir George shouted. "Mr. Harding, this one needs to be disciplined." The merchant pointed indignantly at Squanto. "Clean him up. Then we'll introduce him to the English public."

* * *

The finer element of the English public filled the balconies and stalls of an open-air theater. These sophisticated ladies and gentlemen eagerly watched the bloody spectacle of a pack of dogs attacking a chained bear in a pit.

The audience shouted and flirted, placed bets, drank, and bought Spanish oranges. Sir George sat like a queen bee in the middle of it all, enjoying himself immensely. The big, brown bear roared and batted at the hounds, hurting them badly.

When the bear had defeated the last of the dogs, Sir George signaled to Mr. Harding, then stood and addressed the audience. "Ladies and gentlemen! For your sporting pleasure, the next match has never been seen on English shores. Courtesy of the Plymouth Shipping Company, of which I am proprietor, I present to you . . . a wild barbarian from the New World!"

A great gasp rose from the perfumed horde as Squanto was shoved to the edge of the pit. Ladies screamed. Gentlemen exclaimed. All were thrilled.

Squanto caught just a glimpse of this amazing tribe in its bright colors and frilly lace before he was pushed into the pit. He fell heavily on his back and hadn't even caught his breath when he saw the bear lunging at him.

Here, at last, was something familiar! And though it was brown and not black, like the bears Squanto had hunted in the forests of home, the warrior felt his strength return at the sight of the ferocious beast.

The pale people shrieked and jeered. Squanto clung to the edge of the pit and swatted the bear's tender nose, which sent it yelping back. But the maddened, wounded beast always attacked again.

The pale people slapped their hands together in a loud rhythm, like beavers signaling danger by slapping their leathery tails on a log. Squanto could not understand why they made this noise.

While the warrior was distracted, the bear slapped Squanto hard, knocking him to the ground. The warrior was cornered. He felt the bear's hot breath as it swiped with its deadly claws. The crowd's savage roar drowned out the animal's.

The bear was tied to a stake, but Squanto knew he had to act quickly to save his life. Then an idea came to him: he began *singing* to the bear!

A hush fell over the crowd as his strong voice rose in a haunting Pawtuxet song. The song lulled and hypnotized the beast, and Squanto climbed to his feet. The people and the bear were utterly still.

Suddenly Squanto dived behind the bear and yanked the stake from the ground!

Now shrieks of a different sort echoed over the pit as the big, brown bear shambled over to the edge and climbed into the audience. While the terrified crowd scattered this way and that like startled quail, Squanto escaped!

"My Indian!" Sir George wailed. "Get him! He's a gold mine! Squant*oooo*!" The fat man waddled frantically toward the pit.

He suddenly found himself face-to-snout with the huge, shaggy killer! Sir George turned on his high heels and scampered back up to the balcony.

While the merchant cowered behind a pole, Epenow knocked down his guards. Squanto fought his way through a panic-stricken herd of Englishmen to reach his comrade. Then together the warriors climbed to the upper level of the strange long house. Bullets splintered wood beside them.

Harding shot at the warriors from below, but Sir George screamed, "Don't kill them! I want them alive!"

Hard-shelled soldiers closed in on Squanto and Epenow from all directions. The warriors ran through a door and up a spiral staircase, higher and higher, until they reached an opening.

In pursuit, Harding gasped as the two fugitives leaped through a window into open space! He fired his pistol at his rapidly vanishing prey.

One lead ball punched into Epenow's leg as he and Squanto fell through a straw roof into a room full of hay and squawking birds. Squanto rolled to his feet, but Epenow could not rise. "Go, Squanto, save yourself. Let one of us be free," the warrior commanded, pushing Squanto away.

The enemy was closing in. As he ran, Squanto risked one last look back at his friend. The pale soldiers pounced on Epenow like wolves on a wounded stag.

Squanto ran through the strange village. Their vast wigwams were crammed together. The paths between them were covered with hard, round stones. Great beasts like moose with no antlers pulled huge baskets on things that rolled.

But Squanto did not have time to look at

it all. He was running for his life. People
shrieked. Dogs barked. Squanto knocked
over anything that stood in his way,
scattering all manner of odd objects. He
heard hunting dogs baying behind him.

Squanto's eyes caught the glimmer of
water from the nearby docks. He must reach
the sea before the dogs and shouting soldiers
reached him!

Squanto jumped into the sea.

* * *

"Find him! Look everywhere!" Harding
barked at his men as the wind whipped black
clouds over the bay. A spring storm was
coming. Sea gulls shrieked and wheeled as
they flew to shelter.

Bloodhounds sniffed around crates and
barrels stacked on the crowded dock.
Soldiers poked and prodded at bundles.

"Harding, where are they?" Sir George
demanded, galloping up on a fine horse. His
splendid clothes were a mess, his hair a
jumble of limp curls.

"We've captured one of them, Sir
George," Harding reported.

The merchant barely glanced at Epenow.
The bleeding warrior was held roughly by
two armored soldiers.

"It's the other one I want," Sir George said impatiently. The horse stamped and whinnied. Distant thunder rumbled. "Where's Squanto?"

Thomas Dermer hurried to Epenow and shoved a soldier aside. "This man is wounded. Let go of him. Out of the way!"

Dermer ripped his sleeve to make a bandage and tried to bind Epenow's wound. But the warrior trusted no one, and he kicked Dermer.

"You treat them as human beings. That's your problem," Sir George spat. "Harding! I want Squanto! I will have him, no matter how many men it takes!"

Harding saluted. "Yes, Sir!"

Sir George fumed. "Bloody savage! Thinks he can outwit me! This is England! Find him, Mr. Harding. Find Squanto!"

Lightning flashed and thunder boomed. Sir George reared his horse and furiously galloped away.

* * *

Hoofbeats echoed over the water, along with the barking of many dogs. Squanto crawled from beneath the dock and slipped into a flat-bottomed canoe. Choppy water lapped at the sides of the boat.

Squanto paddled with all his might. But as the storm lashed the wild waves, the canoe dipped and spun out of control. The long paddles were wrenched from his grip. Then a wave swamped the canoe. Squanto was hurled against the wooden sides. He felt his arm snap before he was washed overboard.

The canoe smashed against sharp rocks and shattered. Despite the terrible pain in his arm, Squanto struggled to keep his head above the dark, churning waters. But soon all grew dark.

CHAPTER

4

▼▲▼▲▼▲▼▲▼

When Squanto woke, he was in a place as strange as any he'd seen. He heard chanting. He was lying on a padded platform under a blanket. He was draped in an odd garment, which he ripped off with his good hand. Pain shot through his wounded arm, which was bound in a splint.

Following the sound of the rhythmic chanting, Squanto hobbled to a window. He smashed the latch and opened the shutters. Beyond, he saw fields and trees.

Ignoring his pain, Squanto climbed through the opening, determined to escape. He dropped to the roof of a nearby lodge that smelled of animals.

He heard a man shouting, and the chanting stopped. Squanto jumped off the roof to the ground and found himself surrounded by men completely covered by brown blankets. Their faces were hidden in deep hoods. To his relief, Squanto saw that these Englishmen held no weapons. Then one of the men spoke.

"Give him space, Brother," said the monk Daniel. He pulled back his hood and smiled kindly at the bizarre man he and Brothers Timothy and James had found washed up on the beach the night before. The stranger had inspired much debate in the monastery. By his clothes, they knew the wounded man was no Englishman. But they had no idea what he was.

Brother Paul glared angrily and scolded, "Brother Daniel!"

Paul was in charge of the monastery, and he wanted no part of the peculiar man. In fact, Brother Paul suspected the being was some sort of devil. He had already convinced some of the other monks that this was true.

However, Daniel's kindness had prevailed, and the monks had cared for the unfortunate stranger. Brother Daniel ignored Paul and spoke gently to Squanto. "Go, my friend. You are free."

Brother Daniel stepped back to make a space for Squanto to pass. The warrior was confused, but stumbled toward a distant hill.

"He won't get far," Brother Paul observed. "He's injured and weak."

Daniel smiled slyly. "He's the devil, Brother Paul. You said so yourself. Do I hear sympathy in your voice?"

Brother Paul huffed and crossed his arms. The other monks watched Squanto's wobbly progress, while Daniel fetched a horse from the stables.

Brother Daniel soon caught up with Squanto, who stood at the edge of a cliff, staring sadly out to sea. There was nowhere for him to go.

Heavy wing beats stroked the air high above Squanto's head. He looked up and saw the noble form of a hawk. Daniel dismounted as the other monks approached on foot.

Squanto called out to the hawk, and raised a stone in both hands. The hawk circled, then perched on the stone.

Fat Brother Timothy cried out, "A miracle!"

Brother Paul scowled. "Don't be foolish. That's not a miracle. Come. Back to our prayers."

But the monks ignored Paul, captivated by the spectacle of Squanto and the wild hawk. Daniel's horse suddenly trotted to Squanto, startling the hawk into flight. The warrior tried to stand up, but fainted. Daniel's horse sniffed at Squanto as the monks ran to his aid.

"I told you he is too weak," Brother Paul fussed.

The Brothers carried Squanto back to their monastery. The warrior lay unconscious on a bed of straw while the monks prepared their supper.

Brother Daniel took a bottle of brandy from a shelf. "One of God's creatures came down from the sky to this man. He is no evil beast," Daniel said to Brother Paul.

"Not evil, perhaps, but a beast nonetheless," Paul argued.

"Nonsense. Only so long as we treat him like a beast."

Brother Paul frowned. "Are you suggesting that he eat in here with us?"

"That would spoil my appetite," Brother Timothy objected, ladling stew into bowls. The other monks laughed.

Daniel poked Timothy's fat belly. "Not the worst thing that could happen to you. I suggest that we do not judge this fellow. We should observe him and show him the kindness we would any stranger. Then we may discover who he is."

Brother Paul was stubborn. "He can't even speak!"

"Then I shall teach him to speak." Brother Daniel was equally stubborn, in his own gentle way. He poured a sip of brandy through Squanto's lips. The strong liquid revived the warrior.

The monks backed away when Squanto sat up. Daniel took a bowl of stew from Timothy's hands and set it near the warrior.

"Food," Daniel said. "Food. That is our word for it: food." Brother Daniel stepped away to join the other monks at their long table. Squanto took the bowl of warm stew, but before he could take a bite, Brother Paul knocked on the table three times. Squanto was surprised by the sudden noise.

"We thank Thee, Father, for these and all Thy mercies," Paul intoned.

And the monks replied, "Amen."

Squanto realized the Englishmen were praying. This he understood. Then he ate.

* * *

"I'm tired of hearing 'no'! No! No! No! I'd like to hear 'yes' for a change, Mr. Harding. Do you understand?" Sir George was in a very bad mood. His bulldogs snored in an uneasy heap at his feet. Their stubby legs twitched as they anxiously dreamed.

"Yes, Sir George." Mr. Harding fidgeted like a schoolboy called before the schoolmaster in the luxurious office of the owner of the Plymouth Shipping Company.

"An Indian with hair to the ground and a necklace of shells and feathers disappears in a civilized city. And well-paid, well-trained military men can't find him! It's not like searching for a needle in a haystack. It *is* a haystack!" Sir George ranted.

The dogs woke, ears alert to their master's distress. Sir George snapped his fingers, and a servant handed him a crystal glass of fine sherry.

"Some of us believe he drowned that night in the storm," Harding suggested.

Sir George paced around his desk, sipping sherry. Dogs scrambled out of his way. "I don't accept that theory. I don't like it, either. I want my Indian. I've made promises to London."

Harding did his best to calm his employer. "But you have other savages, Sir. And they are very popular . . ."

Sir George's fat finger jabbed Harding's chest, emphasizing each word. "I am not satisfied with popular. I want *sensational*. Squanto was sensational. He could fight. He could sing. The public clamors to see him again. I invested in that Indian and I want him back. I don't care if the search takes you all the way to Scotland. I want my Squanto!"

* * *

At that moment, Squanto was watching the hornless "deer" the monks kept in a pen. Back in Plymouth, he had seen other Englishmen sitting on the backs of these large, graceful animals. Squanto's wounds were now almost completely healed. With his health, his curiosity had returned. He would have many tales to add to the wampung belt, if he ever found his way home again.

Squanto stared at the big, glossy beasts and remembered a tale of the Pawtuxet.

"*Maushop*," he said.

"What is that?" Daniel asked. "Is that maushop?" The monk followed the warrior's intent gaze. "Horse," said Daniel. "This is a horse. Maushop. Horse. We ride the horse. Let me show you."

Daniel mounted the horse and rode bareback in a circle around Squanto. Daniel dismounted, holding the horse by its mane. "Now you try," he encouraged Squanto.

The warrior skeptically took hold of the animal's long hair and copied the monk's movements. He swung up onto the horse's back.

Daniel laughed with delight. "Ha, ha! You're an excellent student. Horse," he repeated. "Our word is horse."

Squanto repeated, "Horse."

Daniel laughed again. "Yes, you said it. Horse!"

Squanto straightened up. From his position on the animal's strong back he could see far across the fields. This was fun! "Horse!" he shouted happily.

The warrior's shout startled the horse, who suddenly galloped off. Squanto was stunned, but clung to the horse's mane, even as it leaped the fence that bordered the monastery's land.

Squanto had no idea how to stop the huge animal, which ran with the speed of a deer and the strength of a bear. At the edge of a pond, the horse stopped, but Squanto didn't. He flew over the horse's head and splashed into the water!

Squanto emerged with a lily pad flung across his scalp like a hat. Ducks and geese squawked around him, and a pretty pale woman gaped in amazement at his bare chest and unusual clothes. Squanto felt completely foolish in front of this lovely woman, and chose to walk back to his horse as if nothing had happened. The woman smiled at Squanto as he rode away.

* * *

Brother Paul grumbled. "That's what you get for your trust, Brother Daniel. He's a horse thief."

Just then, Squanto and his horse came thundering back to the monastery.

"He's coming back!" Timothy shrieked in alarm.

Monks dived out of the path of the galloping horse. Squanto squeezed the animal's sides with his knees and brought the beast expertly to a halt. "Horse," he said, proud of his new accomplishment.

"He learns fast!" Daniel exclaimed.

Paul scowled.

* * *

"Book!" Squanto repeated.

"Excellent!" Brother Daniel approved. He was showing Squanto the large library where other monks were bending over thick books, dutifully copying them in perfect handwriting. Candlelight reflected on beautiful stained-glass windows.

Daniel realized their lesson was

disturbing his brothers. He led Squanto to a desk away from the others and carefully opened a big leather-bound book.

"Now, I happen to be a man who's read far too many books," Daniel continued in a whisper. "My head is full of all kinds of nonsense, my boy. But I love books. I love everything about them. Let me show you."

Squanto didn't understand what the gentle man was saying. But he sensed Daniel's friendly intentions, and he saw how much the man respected this . . . book. Squanto realized the book was like a wampung belt. It held the stories of this pale tribe and had beautiful pictures. One of the pictures was a woman with soft, dark eyes like those of Squanto's far-off bride.

"Nakooma," Squanto said sadly.

"Nakooma? This one?" Daniel asked. "Is that your word for woman?"

Squanto touched the hawk feather in his hair that Nakooma had given him. "Nakooma." Speaking her name opened a world of sadness in his homesick heart.

Daniel sensed that sadness and said, "I'm going to teach you my language and learn yours if I can. If I can discover where in this vast world you came from, perhaps I can help you go home."

Squanto knew by the sound of the man's

voice that he had found a friend he could trust.

* * *

Soon Squanto became part of life at the monastery. Though Brother Paul was less than pleased, Squanto broke bread with them at the long table, like all the others.

Squanto helped the monks clear a field. He fished with timid Brother James at the shore where he had been found after the storm. And all the while, Squanto learned the English tongue and showed the more open-minded monks something of his own ways. Fat Brother Timothy liked the soft, comfortable moccasins Squanto made for him, even though they got him in trouble with Brother Paul. But Paul was helpless to stop the trend. Soon all the Brothers were wearing the soft, deerskin shoes.

There came a day when the leaves were changing color and the birds were flying south. Squanto felt winter in the air and knew he had been gone from his home for an entire year.

To keep his sadness at bay, Squanto taught the Brothers to play lacrosse. With their heavy brown robes tucked up, the monks tumbled and skidded across the field in their comfortable moccasins. They hacked at the gourd "ball" with their netted sticks. They laughed like boys. Even Brother Timothy joined in.

But Paul disapproved. He watched from a distance, pruning leaves in his garden. Daniel reluctantly left the game to speak with the monastery's leader.

"We are forgetting our purpose here," Brother Paul said.

"There's nothing sinful in this," said Daniel.

Paul disagreed. "Your pagan friend has disrupted our quiet life. It's time he left."

"But he can't leave," Daniel objected. "He's . . . still recovering from his injuries."

Brother Paul raised an eyebrow. In the field, Squanto leaped and ran ahead of a pack of pursuing monks. "I'm not a doctor, Brother Daniel. But I daresay he's recovered." Paul returned to his gardening.

"But he's learning from us," Daniel said. "He's beginning to speak and observe our ways. Is it not our duty to bring light into the darkness?"

Paul pointed to a wilted plant. "Do you see this flower? It is a yellow narcissus. When it blooms, its petals look like a trumpet. But it isn't blooming because it's a gift from our brothers in a monastery in

France. You see? You can't uproot a flower and plant it in a place where it doesn't belong. This yellow narcissus will wither and die."

Brother Daniel did not disagree. But he said, "Squanto has nowhere to go. He's lost. And from what he's told me, I believe he's come from the New World . . ."

"Poppycock!" Paul exclaimed. "I'll never believe it. There is no New World. There's only this world. And this world, Brother Daniel, is flat!"

Daniel sighed. "Oh, Brother Paul."

"Flat!"

A sudden rain drove the lacrosse players back into the monastery. Brother Daniel raised his hood. "Whatever you believe, Squanto came to our country by ship. Winter is upon us, and no ships will sail before spring. Would you deny him shelter, Brother Paul?"

The rain fell harder, splattering on leaves, stone, and earth. Paul grumbled and pulled up his own hood. The two monks followed the players into the monastery.

CHAPTER

5

▼▲▼▲▼▲▼

Rain and snow drenched the streets of Plymouth Harbor. Harding's soldiers huddled around the fireplace in the Plymouth Shipping Company's warehouse. Epenow squatted, bound in a dark corner. Though captive, the Nausett sachem watched and heard everything around him. His eyes glittered like a caged panther's. Nearby, Thomas Dermer took inventory of the company's goods.

"Four months and still no sign of him," Sir George complained to Mr. Harding. The rich merchant was followed around by a servant carrying a silver tray of food. The man struggled not to trip over his employer's pack of bulldogs.

"He must have drowned, Sir. It's the only explanation."

"That's a convenient explanation, Mr. Harding. If he's dead, give me proof," Sir George demanded.

Desperately, Harding said, "Look at my men. The weather's been fierce. They've been frostbitten. We've lost two horses."

Sir George did not care. "If you fail me, you'll lose your position, your status, your reputation, your future." The dogs growled and yapped. Sir George stopped and looked at two men standing in the door. Rain was dripping from their plain cloaks and broad-brimmed hats. "Who are you?" he asked.

The men stepped forward, with nervous glances at the bulldogs. The first said, "Sir George, my name is William Bradford and this is Dr. Samuel Fuller."

Sir George eyed their dark, plain clothing. "Puritans," he said with a sneer.

Bradford began, "Several of us would like to book passage on one of your ships."

"We seek religious freedom," Dr. Fuller added.

Sir George had no patience for these fanatics with their boring devotion to morality. "I'm not opposed to shipping you and your fanatical lot across the sea. But I don't deal in shillings, gentlemen. I deal in pounds."

"We have very little, I'm afraid," Bradford admitted.

"Then, gentlemen, you're wasting my valuable time," Sir George replied with a wave of his chubby hand. His gold ring sparkled in the dim light. "Mr. Dermer, come into my office, please."

Dermer obediently followed Sir George and the tray-bearing servant who walked amid the yapping pack. Harding turned to the two Puritans. "You're wasting your own time as well," he told them. "The New World is not a place for . . . men of peace. You won't survive without military protection."

"We have our faith and are resolute in our purpose," Dr. Fuller said firmly.

Harding smiled slyly and tapped his pistol. "It will take more than that, my friend." He walked away.

Bradford and Fuller disagreed with the British officer, but worry nibbled at their beliefs.

* * *

Sir George nibbled at the delicacies beneath the silver covers of the trays. He tossed choice tidbits to his bulldogs. "Dermer, you're a man of maps and charts.

Take a look at this map of England. Where would Squanto go?"

The merchant unrolled a large map. Dermer studied it. "Where he comes from, his tribe dwells by the ocean, so I doubt he'd go inland," Dermer proposed. "Not near any cities, certainly. They would only terrify him."

Sir George cast a shrewd eye at Dermer. "You know all about these chaps, don't you?"

"I believe if we want to trade with them we must learn all we can about their culture," Dermer explained.

Sir George popped a small potato in his mouth. The bulldogs' eyes followed every motion of his hands. "I can't imagine anything more tedious."

"It's practical, Sir George," Dermer stated. "It's good business. By stealing these men from their tribes, you've destroyed many future opportunities. You've made enemies instead of friends. You cannot conduct business with enemies, Sir."

"But we're stronger than they are. They'll do whatever we want," Sir George replied.

"You watched Squanto fight off a squadron of armed men. These are not complacent people, Sir. They are warriors."

Sir George didn't like what he was hearing. But Dermer's words made sense. The merchant toyed with his gold ring, then reached a decision. "Do you consider yourself competent enough to master one of my ships?"

Dermer was surprised. "More than competent, Sir!"

"I will place you in command of the *Archangel* on her next expedition abroad," Sir George declared.

Dermer was in shock. This was a dream come true! He managed to say, "Thank you, Sir George." Then he left the room elated, pinching himself to make sure he was awake.

Sir George lifted the largest tray cover and sniffed. "Mmm. Pork pie. Why anyone would want to leave England, I'll never know!"

* * *

Brother Paul surveyed the men sitting around the long monastery table. Squanto sat among them, dressed in warm English clothes, but with the hawk feather still stuck in his long, black hair. A winter wind howled around the walls. The pounding surf of the nearby ocean roared like an angry bear.

Paul bowed his head. "Heavenly Father,

we thank Thee for these and all Thy blessings. Amen."

At the same time, Squanto said a prayer in his own language. "Creator, thank you for the food which we are now going to sit down and eat."

"Amen," said the monks.

"Kissuulk," said Squanto.

Brother Paul's eyes snapped open. "What is that word?"

Brother Daniel answered, "It is the name of Squanto's God."

"I see. And what exactly is the function of . . . Squanto's God?" Paul was suspicious. He would have no pagan worship in his monastery!

"Squanto, tell us about Kissuulk," Daniel prompted.

Squanto said, "He is the creator."

Paul could not think of anything to say, so he picked up his spoon and began to eat. So did the other monks.

In a moment, Paul said, "I must say, Daniel, you've made progress in your attempt to educate our . . . guest. He's learning our language, and he's learned some manners too."

"Courtesy and respect for ritual and prayer are as important to his people as they are to ours," Daniel said mildly.

Paul nodded, then said, "Squanto, this mysterious land that you come from, you must miss it after all this time."

Squanto considered Paul's words. First he had to grasp the English, then form a reply. "Yes, Brother Paul. I miss my family, my people, and Nakooma."

Paul looked at Daniel. "Nakooma?"

"Nakooma is the name of Squanto's bride," Daniel explained.

Paul's eyes raised. "Bride? You're married?"

The monks exclaimed, "How wonderful! What a surprise! Any children?"

Squanto looked around at the excited men. For the first time he thought to ask them, "Where are the women of *your* tribe?"

The monks fell silent. A few spoons froze between bowls and open mouths. Paul looked at Daniel, who answered, "We have no women, Squanto. We have devoted our lives to God."

"Your tribe will die with no women," Squanto said sensibly.

"We are not a tribe," Paul declared firmly.

To Squanto, a group of people who lived, worked, prayed, and ate together were a tribe. "I would never join a tribe without women," the Pawtuxet stated.

Brother Paul repeated, "We are not a . . ."

But by now Squanto was lost in his own thoughts. "I loved Nakooma when Nakooma and Squanto were children," he said. He was suddenly homesick, and finished speaking in Algonquin.

Daniel had to translate. "He says, 'Men came to my village and stole me on the day I was to begin my bridal journey.'"

"What is a bridal journey?" Paul asked.

Squanto did not answer, because he was gripped with a sudden realization. "My father told me to go with Nakooma. I did not obey my father. I did not obey the ways of my people. Kissuulk punished me."

Suddenly feeling very sad, he got up from the table and wandered out into the cold night. The moaning wind seemed to echo the terrible emptiness in his aching heart. The snow and everything before his tear-filled eyes reminded Squanto of home. Then a hawk flapped its powerful wings before landing near him.

CHAPTER

6

The hawk soared high in the clear, blue sky. Spring had come at last, and with it, flowers and green grass and the sun. The hawk landed in a tree. Daniel and Squanto rode horses on the edge of the cliff by the sea. Daniel looked up at the hawk and said in Algonquin, "*Bibougest.*"

"Yes, hawk," Squanto agreed. "Beautiful hawk. My friend, my protector. He is always with me."

Daniel smiled. "You've learned my language much better than I've learned yours."

"For me there was no choice," Squanto said. "Was there, Maushop?" He patted the horse's neck.

Daniel nodded. "I've never understood your word for horse. Maushop. Your people have no horses, you said."

"My father told me stories of the great beast Maushop. He said it will one day come out of the sea," Squanto explained. He gazed across the sea and remembered wise Mooshawset.

Suddenly the hawk took flight and flapped across their path. Squanto stopped Maushop and became very still.

"What is it?" Daniel asked.

"The hawk crossed our path. He warns us. Listen." Squanto heard a sound and cautiously rode toward it, following the hawk.

Cresting a hill, Squanto slipped off Maushop's back and tied the horse to a tree. He crept like a hunter and hid on the ridge of the hill. Daniel awkwardly followed the warrior.

Down below was the farm pond where Squanto had splashed on his first day of riding. Soldiers were speaking to the pretty young woman. The woman seemed reluctant to answer, but the heavily armed men surrounded her. At last, she pointed up to the monastery.

The soldiers remounted and rode away. As they passed close, Daniel lifted his head. "Who are they?"

Squanto pushed the monk to the ground. He had recognized Harding as the leader. The approaching hoofbeats drummed the hillside.

Daniel's heart drummed with fear. Panic overtook him. Squanto tried to calm his companion, but could not restrain the frightened monk. Daniel leaped up. "We must go back!"

Brother Daniel bolted for his horse, and the soldiers saw him. Squanto had intended to remain hidden, but he was now in the path of the horsemen pursuing the monk. He had no choice. Dodging from rock to bush, Squanto reached Maushop and galloped after the fearful monk. They did not stop until they were in the woods. Brother Daniel cried, "Go on, Squanto. Hide from them! Hurry!"

The warrior turned his horse and rode deeper into the woods. Daniel waited until he heard the soldiers nearby. Then he rode quickly back to the monastery.

* * *

The sound of clattering hooves startled Brother Paul. He put down a potted flower and hastened from the prayer garden only to see Daniel's horse race into the quiet courtyard.

"What is the meaning . . . ?" Paul sputtered.

"We have no time to quarrel," Daniel said breathlessly. "They've come looking for Squanto."

Curious monks trotted into the courtyard. They saw the soldiers charging the gate. Brother Paul said, "Perhaps he belongs with the authorities."

"His spirit will die in captivity. We mustn't tell them he's here," Daniel urged. The soldiers drew closer.

"Don't ask me to lie," Paul said firmly. "I will not lie."

"Then do not speak at all!" Daniel snapped.

Harding and his soldiers reined their frothing horses. "You there!" Harding shouted. "You're holding property that does not belong to you."

"You, Sir, are standing on private ground," Daniel said calmly.

"We know he's here, Friar. Hand him over. He's owned by the Plymouth Shipping Company."

"The Plymouth Shipping Company has no business in this sanctuary," Daniel countered.

"This sanctuary, by Protestant law, has no business in England!" Harding replied. He waved his arm. "Search!"

The soldiers drew their swords with a ring of steel. The rough men stormed the sanctuary, shoving Daniel and the other monks out of the way. One trooper rode into the orderly prayer garden and hacked down plants and flowers. Pots shattered and soil spilled.

Brother Paul flinched as if struck in the face. "My flowers! Stop!"

Concealed by the budding branches of a nearby grove of trees, Squanto saw all that happened. He could not let the soldiers destroy this tribe that had given him shelter.

He tied Maushop to a tree and crept toward the monastery, staying low and ducking behind cover. Squanto heard pots crashing in the monastery kitchen, and doors kicked open. He seethed with anger.

Squanto looked up and saw the hawk crying on the rooftop. He prepared to leap into battle. But a hand clasped his shoulder. He turned and saw Brother James.

"No, Squanto, it's you they're after. Stay hidden," the shy monk advised.

But every muscle in Squanto's body longed for the fight. These soldiers had no right to destroy this village!

Cautiously, Squanto glided along a wall toward a small window in the library. Brother James followed.

At the window, Squanto saw soldiers burst into the tidy library. The troopers threw books to the floor and kicked over the copy desks. Inkwells splashed on the stone floor. Harding knocked over a bookstand, and a Bible flopped like a dead bird onto the hard floor.

"Stop! What is the purpose of all this

destruction?" Brother Daniel asked from the doorway.

"Speed! I'm out of patience with this bloody Indian," Harding snarled. He kicked over a table of delicate bookbindings.

"These are our books, our manuscripts!" Daniel cried. He stepped between Harding and a shelf of priceless illustrated books.

"Out of the way, monk!" Harding barked.

Daniel was defiant. "I will not!"

"Out of my way, I said!" Harding shoved the monk hard.

But Daniel stood up again. "This is our place of learning."

"Then let me teach you!" Harding growled, and he shoved Daniel harder, slamming him against a table.

Again, Daniel stood up. Harding punched him with all of his anger and strength. "The sooner you cooperate, the sooner we'll stop." Harding threw Daniel aside. He seized a book and pitched it through the stained-glass window. The colored glass shattered like a rainbow dissolving in the sky.

Squanto was about to leap when he heard Brother Paul say, "We will cooperate."

Everyone turned to look at the monastery's leader. Paul said quietly, "Tell me what you want."

Harding swaggered up. "You know what

we want, Friar. The beast. The wild Indian that lives like a filthy animal. The savage."

Brother Paul looked from the broken window to Harding. "Savage?" he asked innocently. "Beast? Filthy animal?" Paul stooped and lifted the fallen Bible from the floor. "I swear upon this Holy Book, no one like that is here."

Harding glared into Paul's eyes. Then he angrily signaled to his men. The soldiers followed Harding out the door.

Daniel sagged against the wall. All the monks sighed with relief as the soldiers' horses trotted away.

As soon as they were gone, the Brothers set about cleaning up the mess. Squanto quietly entered the library. "You protected me, all of you. They did this to you, your books, your house. All this happened because of me."

"No, Squanto," Daniel said. "This happened because there are some people who bully their way through this world with cruelty and force."

Squanto knew this was true. The Pawtuxets had often been raided by greedy neighbors. But Squanto was baffled. "And you have no weapons to stop them?"

"That is not how we battle our enemies," Paul told him.

Squanto pointed around the room at the broken desks and ruined books. "Enemies destroy you."

"Our books and windows, yes," Paul conceded. "But our spirits are still intact."

Daniel set up the Bible stand. Squanto stooped to help, picking up broken pieces. "You do not hate the men who did this?" he asked the monks.

"Hatred only leads to more hatred," Daniel stated firmly.

Squanto recognized the wisdom in those words. He admired the monks' dignity and the strength of their faith. He understood now that they were men of peace. Their refusal to fight was not cowardice but courage.

"Brothers, they will not give up their search," Timothy said sadly. "They will come back."

"I cannot stay here," said Squanto.

Daniel made a decision. "We must help you go home. Now that spring has come, we must learn of any ships departing from England. When you go to market in the village, Brothers, ask of any news."

"Brothers, thank you," Squanto said. "You are warriors."

And together, Squanto and his Brothers finished cleaning up their home.

CHAPTER

7

▼△▼△▼△▼△▼△▼

"Humpty Dumpty sat on a wall.
Humpty Dumpty had a great fall.
All the King's horses and all the
    King's men
Couldn't put Humpty together again."

Epenow spoke the odd English rhyme
with great dignity. Despite his chains and
leather bindings, he was still a sachem of the
Nausetts.

Sir George paced before the warrior,
bulldogs circling his feet. The merchant
anxiously twisted his big gold ring. He
tapped the ring against his front tooth. "He's
making progress," Sir George said to his

servant. "But he's nothing like the one that got away."

"Squanto the Savage. His escape from the bear pit has become a bit of a legend around here," the servant agreed.

Sir George squinted at the man. "When people tell the story, am I depicted as an object of ridicule?"

"Of course not, Sir!" the servant said hastily.

Suddenly the doors burst open, and Harding strode into the Plymouth Shipping Company warehouse. "Sir George, I bring you news of your savage. He's been seen a mere thirty miles from here!"

"He's alive?" Sir George could hardly believe his ears. The bulldogs cocked their heads.

"Yes, Sir. We've not captured him yet. He eluded us. But we'll find him in time," Harding said with determination.

Sir George beamed with excitement. "Good work, Harding! But let's quicken the time, shall we?" The merchant turned to his servant. "Announce to the city the return of Squanto the Savage! Make it widely known that Squanto will perform on stage at the Swan Theater before a month has passed."

Sir George made a grand, sweeping gesture, then suddenly stopped. "My ring! It's gone!"

Sir George's head whipped around from side to side, looking for the thief. Epenow held out his fist and slowly opened it. He held the gold ring.

"Gold," he said.

"Give me that, you wretched thief! I'll have you shot!" Sir George shrieked. The dogs barked in alarm.

Fixing the merchant with his panther eyes, Epenow said coolly, "My land. Gold. We have much gold. Everywhere gold."

Then, as if the ring were a speck of nothing, Epenow tossed it back and crossed his arms with patient confidence, like a fisherman sure of his bait.

Sir George snatched his precious ring from the air. Epenow's words had hooked his greedy, selfish nature. Gold! Could it really be that this savage came from a land covered with gold?

Sir George grabbed his servant. "I must speak with Mr. Dermer at once."

In his eagerness, Sir George didn't even mind that Mr. Dermer was aboard the *Archangel*. Sir George swallowed his distaste for ships and hurried to the harbor. He was in such a rush he left his bulldogs behind.

The bustling crew stopped work and saluted at the sudden appearance of their employer. Sir George nodded vacantly at this tribute.

Dermer greeted the merchant politely. "Welcome aboard, Sir George. The *Archangel* has been maintained and prepared. She'll be ready to sail as planned."

"Good, good, very good," the rich man said mechanically. Then he pulled Dermer away from the sailors. His voice dropped to a whisper. "To be perfectly honest, I find boats to be rather squalid, even when they're seaworthy. I prefer solid ground: my office, my carriage, my ledger, my servants, my dogs. I've come on business and I'd like to make this quick."

"As you wish, Sir," said Dermer.

Sir George looked around to make sure no one else was listening. "My Indian, Epenow, says there's gold in his country. Opinion?"

"It's a vast and wondrous place, Sir. It's very possible," Dermer said thoughtfully.

It was Sir George's turn to think. Then he said, "If I send him with you, could you persuade him to lead you to the gold?"

"Perhaps in exchange for his freedom," Dermer replied. "And I could use him to help me trade with his people again."

Sir George rubbed his chubby hands with glee. This was all working out even better than he'd hoped! "I'd let Epenow go, if I could be certain of replacing him with Squanto."

"Squanto's been located, I've heard," Dermer said carefully.

"Located but not caught. We need to lure him back somehow," said Sir George. His mind was busy calculating profits, losses, methods, and means.

Dermer was a little sarcastic when he answered, "What in our culture could possibly attract him?"

The irony of the man's remark was lost on his employer. "Everybody wants something," said Sir George. "And if you can figure out what a person wants most, you can get him to do anything for it." He pondered the problem. "What do you suppose Squanto wants more than anything in the world?"

Dermer said dryly, "The same thing Epenow wants — to go home."

Sir George's face lit with glee. "Brilliant! We'll let it be known in every village between here and Cornwall that this ship is sailing to the New World. And then we'll wait."

Business concluded, Sir George hurried off the dreadful ship as fast as his short legs would carry him.

"Squanto! Squanto!"

Squanto raised his head at the sound of Brother Timothy's voice. The Pawtuxet was tending the flowers in the prayer garden, repairing the damage done by Harding's soldiers.

"Here, Brother Timothy," Squanto said, wiping his soiled hands. He saw James pulling a wooden cart behind the swiftly waddling Brother.

The fat monk was so excited and out of breath from running, he could barely talk. Timothy puffed and gasped. "We . . . a ship . . . we . . ."

"What is it, Timothy?" Brother Daniel asked as he approached.

Other monks gathered around the excited Brother. Timothy's mouth moved like a fish out of water, but he couldn't catch his breath. Brother James spoke instead. "We've been to the market and learned of a ship that's leaving Plymouth in fifteen days."

Daniel rejoiced at the news, but caution tempered his happiness. "What ship?"

"It's called the *Archangel*. It's owned by the Plymouth Shipping Company," James reported.

Daniel knew the name well. He said to

Squanto, "The Plymouth Shipping Company is no friend of yours."

Brother Timothy finally caught his breath. "But all we need to do is get him on board. Daniel, there may not be another ship for months or years!"

"You are tempted, Squanto," Daniel observed.

"My dream to go home is bigger than my fear," the warrior answered.

Daniel considered the situation and spoke to the other monks. "It will not be easy to get him on board — this or any other ship. He is wanted, hunted. He will be noticed in Plymouth."

The others agreed upon the difficulty of the task. But as they discussed it, Brother Paul interrupted.

"What on earth is this?" The senior monk stood by James' cart, examining an ear of corn.

"Food, Brother Paul," James explained shyly. "We bought it at the market."

Paul was baffled. "Food? It's hard as a rock."

James's soft voice went on. "It's been dried. You plant it in the ground."

"A great big thing like this?" Paul was skeptical.

"I believe it grows into an enormous tree," James offered timidly.

Squanto laughed and strode to their side. The familiar vegetable brought with it happy memories of home. When the leaves of the white oak were as big as the ears of a mouse, the women planted corn. Squanto remembered Nakooma leaning on her hoe. First, the news of the ship and now corn. Squanto hoped Kissuulk was speaking to him. Perhaps his time of punishment was near an end!

Squanto took another ear of corn from the cart and stripped off the husk. The monks were impressed by the purple, yellow, and white kernels on the cob.

"Seeds," Squanto said. "These will grow."

He picked off some kernels and knelt on the ground. Squanto had seen Nakooma do this many times. But since this tribe had no women, he would show them how to plant corn.

Squanto poked a hole in the rich soil with his finger and dropped in four kernels: one for each of the four winds. "We should put in a fish head to feed the seeds while they grow."

"How does Squanto know so much about this strange food?" Paul wondered.

James swallowed hard before giving an answer he knew Brother Paul wouldn't like. "It . . . came from the . . . New World."

Paul didn't answer. He stared at this fantastic, knobby thing that was unlike any plant he had ever seen in all his years of gardening. Here was more evidence of the faraway place that couldn't exist. Brother Paul shook his head sadly.

* * *

There was more for Paul to shake his head at later that evening in the monastery kitchen. The monks were gathered around Squanto, who crouched before the fire holding a dish above the flames.

"Brothers, we have not even prayed," Paul scolded.

"Shh! The food is speaking," Squanto said.

Paul huffed. This was too much. "Oh! Food from the New World speaks does it? I doubt—"

POP!

Brother Paul's mouth snapped shut. The amazed monks leaned closer.

POP! A puffed kernel jumped out of the dish. The Brothers gaped in wonder. Then, POP, POP, POP, POP, POP!

The terrified monks stumbled over each other in their eagerness to get away from the noisy flying food! They crouched along the walls, muttering prayers against devils.

Squanto stayed by the fire, holding the dish with a blizzard of popcorn flying around him. He brought the popcorn over to the monks. Squanto took a few kernels in his mouth to show them how to eat it, but the Brothers would have none of it.

"English, English, you have no courage," Squanto teased. He chomped big mouthfuls and laughed at their astonished faces.

Finally, fat Timothy ventured forth, saying a hasty prayer. He ate a mouthful. "Oh, Brothers! It's delicious!" He grabbed another handful.

Then the others tried the new food. Squanto passed the plate among them. When it reached Brother Paul, everyone watched and waited.

The senior monk looked at the popcorn and finally sampled one small piece. He looked at Squanto very seriously and said gruffly, "If such a place of wonders does exist, your heart must ache to go back to it."

Paul turned sternly to Daniel. "Brother Daniel, you have my permission to ride to Plymouth. You will put yourself in danger by doing so. This will by no means be an easy task. But you must see Squanto safely to the ship, and then return."

Brother Timothy spoke around a mouthful of popcorn. "May I go too?"

Paul sighed. "No, Brother Timothy, the city holds too many vile temptations that you would find too hard to resist."

Timothy shrugged and reached for more popcorn. Paul was probably right.

* * *

The next morning, many monks were in the fields planting corn as Squanto had shown them. The warrior himself was with Daniel in the stable. Squanto wore a monk's brown robe. Timothy helped them load supplies on the horses.

The hawk perched on Squanto's arm. The Pawtuxet addressed the bird. "Goodbye, my friend. Now you protect these good men the way you watched over me."

And the hawk flew to the roof of the barn.

Brother Paul called from the prayer garden. "Squanto, I would like to speak to you, please."

Squanto joined the stern leader among his beloved flowers.

"So this is the day you're leaving us," Paul said. "For some here, this will be a sad day. You managed to teach us a thing or two."

"I also learned a thing or two," Squanto said.

A slight smile touched Paul's face. "I daresay you're quite a sight in that sackcloth. Do you feel at all like a monk?"

Squanto considered for a moment, then answered playfully, "I am thinking about a woman, Brother Paul."

Despite himself, the monk laughed. The tiny spark of mirth was quickly extinguished. But he wasn't quite as prickly when he spoke again. "I'll tell you something, Squanto. It's not a bad idea to step inside another person's shoes now and then and see the world from where he stands. I confess it is a stubborn weakness of mine: I resist the possibility of other worlds, of other customs, of other points of view. And I sometimes overlook the goodness in a man even when it's staring me in the face."

Then Paul offered his hand and said, "Go in peace. You have my blessing."

Squanto shook the monk's hand and thanked him. Then he turned to leave.

"Wait!" Paul called after him. "You haven't been fiddling with my flower garden, have you?"

Squanto grinned. "Goodbye, my friend."

Brother Paul picked up a small clay pot that held a flower whose petals formed a delicate yellow trumpet — a blooming yellow narcissus.

CHAPTER

8

▼▲▼▲▼▲▼▲▼

When Squanto and Brother Daniel rode
into Plymouth, they saw a mob harassing a
group of people in dark clothing. Loud voices
yelled, "We don't want you in our city!" and
"Fanatics!" and "Throw them out!"

One of the victims was brutally thrown
onto the cobblestone street. Squanto's first
impulse was to defend the outnumbered man.
"Why do they hurt these people?" he asked.

Brother Daniel said, "The mob does not
tolerate other beliefs."

The victims of the mob were known as
Puritans. Their religious beliefs clashed with
those of the Church of England, which had the
support of the King and the nobility. The

Puritans believed in family prayer, Bible study, and Sunday as a day of rest and meditation. They did not think religion should be confined to a formal church led by professional priests.

"It's not right," said Squanto. "We must help them."

"You must stay hidden," Daniel reminded his friend as he pulled him away from the fight.

A large, bearded man in rich clothing pushed roughly through the crowd to make his way to the fallen Puritan.

"Away! Leave this man alone!" he ordered. The crowd parted like the Red Sea at Moses' command. This was no Biblical prophet, but Miles Standish, who had just been introduced to Dr. Fuller and Mr. Bradford.

The formidable military man had offered his services as protector of the proposed Puritan colony in the New World. Mr. Bradford doubted the military belonged in a community of peace. But Standish had said, "Peace does not exist without security."

The crowd backed away, grumbling and muttering, but offering no further violence. Dr. Fuller was impressed by the way Standish took charge of a potentially dangerous situation. "We will need him, Bradford, if we ever find a ship."

"We must find a ship — and we shall!" Bradford said.

The three men paid no attention to the two brown-robed monks who rode away from the crowd. Squanto and Daniel hadn't gone far before they heard a voice braying, "Inside, Ladies and Gentlemen! Chief Epenow! This brave sachem from the New World will battle the Ottoman Army! The wildest in the world! I warn you, though, this performance is not for the faint of heart."

The speaker stood in front of the Swan Theater, a big, two-story building shaped like a doughnut. The upper level was a balcony of "Lords' Boxes" where the wealthy sat. Poor folk, or the "groundlings," stood shoulder-to-shoulder on the ground level.

Flags flying from the theater's gilded roof announced the performance. Exposed wooden beams supported its white plaster walls, which were decorated with huge posters of the Nausett. Dressed in an outlandish costume, the Epenow on the posters looked like a fierce devil.

Squanto was shocked. Could this be his friend? He turned Maushop and rode to the back entrance of the theater.

Daniel objected, "No, Squanto! It's too dangerous."

"Brother Daniel, I have seen you stand up

to danger. You risked your life for a friend," Squanto recalled. He pointed to the gaudy poster. "Epenow is my friend. I must do the same."

And as he turned his horse, drums and music played inside the theater. The show had already started. Squanto rode around the building looking for a way in.

He found a deserted spot and stroked Maushop's head. The horse became very still. Squanto stood on its back and strained to reach a wooden beam. His hand fell short, so he clicked his tongue and said, "Maushop!"

The horse reared up. Squanto easily reached the rafter and swung upward. From there he climbed over the roof and through the scaffolding.

He saw Epenow down below in a fur robe. The warrior was surrounded by soldiers in gold and red uniforms. His enemies brandished curved swords. Epenow shed his robe and grappled with a soldier.

Squanto thought, *This is worse than the bear.* The Pawtuxet forgot any concern for his own safety. He had to rescue his friend! Squanto pulled off his monk's hood and shrieked a war cry that shook the rafters.

In the audience, Sir George had been content that Epenow had finally submitted. Many whippings had inspired this performance. But this horrible shriek wasn't part of the act!

The crowd roared with delighted surprise. Sir George gasped in amazed triumph as Squanto swung down to the stage. "Ha, ha! The fool walked right into my trap!" Sir George crowed.

Squanto flattened a pair of soldiers. He snatched up a sword and swung at the other three. They timidly backed away, holding up empty hands. They were only actors, not real soldiers. The crowd howled with laughter.

Harding was already rallying his men.

"Take your time," Sir George said, savoring his victory. "He delights the audience."

Squanto lunged at the fake soldiers. He swung the sword, which smashed against a pole and splintered to bits. The blade was made of cheap wood. Squanto did not know what to think.

A boy in the audience cried out, "Squanto the Savage!"

The crowd cheered wildly and stamped their feet. "Squanto! Squanto! Squanto!"

The Pawtuxet warrior was even more confused. Then Harding's soldiers closed in, muskets at the ready. Epenow stepped close to Squanto and said, "You still have not learned, my friend. You must understand your enemy if you wish to defeat him."

Muskets pointed at the warriors from all sides, like the muzzles of a wolf pack. Squanto was again a prisoner.

* * *

Later, Sir George rubbed his fat hands with glee when he had Squanto tied up in his warehouse. "Well now, Squanto, congratulations! You were a spectacle this afternoon. The groundlings loved it. The gentry loved it. You're the talk of the town."

Sir George stepped closer to his bound prisoner. His bulldogs sniffed at the captive warrior. "There is indeed a ship sailing to your homeland. It leaves from Plymouth tomorrow as soon as the winds are right. Your friend Epenow will be on board that ship. You, however, will not."

The merchant suddenly slapped Squanto with the back of his hand. The gold ring stung the warrior's face. "You can't run away from me, Indian," Sir George roared. "I own you. And from this moment on you will do whatever I tell you to do. Comply and you'll be treated reasonably. Defy me, and you'll be punished."

Spittle flew from the rich man's lips. Then he paused and composed himself. On his way to the door, Sir George added, "There is a divine order to life. First, God, followed by the angels, and then the king. The rest of us according to our position in this world. Your position is lower than the animals. Remember that, Squanto. You are not a man. You are livestock."

The door slammed behind him, and the lock clicked shut.

Squanto was beyond rage. He felt devastated, yet he knew he must not give up hope.

Epenow said, "Use your dreams tonight."

"Thank you, nephew," Squanto replied.

* * *

Captain Thomas Dermer was working late. His crew carried cargo up the gangplanks of the *Archangel*. Dermer paced the dock, giving orders and watching sailors heft heavy barrels and crates. Then he noticed someone standing in the shadows. "You there," Dermer said, approaching the stranger.

The newcomer wore a hood and tried to stay hidden in darkness. But Dermer noticed his footwear: moccasins. Although Dermer didn't know who the stranger was, he realized the man somehow knew Squanto. "The man you're looking for is not here, Friar," said Dermer.

Brother Daniel drew back his hood. "Do you know where he is?"

"Locked safely away," Dermer said dryly.

"He'll die if he's trapped and caged! His spirit needs to be free. Is there any way you can help us, Sir?" the monk asked desperately.

Dermer was master of the *Archangel*, and he would not risk losing that position now. "It has nothing to do with me," he replied coldly.

"Yes it has!"

Dermer was surprised by the monk's remark. "In what way?"

"Squanto was stolen from his homeland on a ship like this. It is only right that he be returned," Daniel said.

Dermer felt a pang of guilt, remembering his own part in Squanto's kidnapping. He had not liked it then, and he had doubts now. But he had a duty. "I am master of this ship, but not its owner. I cannot authorize this. I'm sorry."

He turned away, but Daniel was persistent. "Can you tell me when the ship sails?"

"That will be decided by the wind," Dermer said impatiently. "When it is favorable, we will set sail. And we will wait for no one."

The captain of the *Archangel* turned on his heel and strode down the dock.

CHAPTER

9

▼▲▼▲▼▲▼▲▼

Squanto slept badly. His bound hands were stiff and swollen. When the sun came up, a soldier came into the warehouse and left a bowl of gruel at the warrior's feet.

Squanto stared at the pale slop. He was hungry, but he had a better idea. Squanto plunged his hands into the sticky liquid. Then he held his dripping hands close to the wooden wall. Squanto made a tiny noise with his tongue.

Slowly, carefully, cautiously, rats poked their pink snouts from the boards. Sniffing, twitching, twittering, they inched toward the offered feast.

Squanto didn't mind the tiny bites he got.

The hungry rats ate the rope along with the gruel!

* * *

"The *Archangel* has taken on cargo, Sir George, and awaits your orders to set sail," Mr. Harding reported.

The merchant looked up from a ledger book and set down his golden pen. "Splendid! I will arrive at the dock precisely at noon. And, Harding, I would like Squanto to be taken down there as well."

"Squanto, Sir?" Harding was not happy to hear this.

"I want fanfare, publicity, excitement. People look upon the Plymouth Shipping Company as a leader in pioneering ventures, taming and civilizing the faraway world. Put Squanto on display. He'll add to the general amusement."

"Yes, Sir George," Harding said reluctantly.

The merchant leaned forward. "And make very certain that you keep him bound and guarded at all times."

* * *

Harding had no idea how difficult

carrying out that order would be. He checked his pistol before he stepped into the warehouse and barked, "Stand up, savage!"

Squanto would not. When the guards reached for him to drag him out, Squanto sprang up as swiftly as a fox. He was out the door and gone before Harding could blink!

Squanto sprinted through the narrow, crooked streets with soldiers at his heels like a pack of hunting hounds. Citizens screamed when they saw the warrior's streaming hair and hawk feather. Everyone knew Squanto the Savage.

Squanto eluded another pack of soldiers, but now Harding and others on horseback were quickly gaining on him. Harding was close enough to swat Squanto with the flat of his sword.

The warrior stumbled and fell on the hard cobblestones. Pain shot through his hands and up Squanto's strong arms. He would rather die than return to Sir George's clutches.

The soldiers were clumsy in their heavy helmets and breastplates. Squanto scrambled to his feet and dodged between them. The soldiers doubled back to follow him. Squanto ran around a house and down a narrow alley, then stopped dead. The soldiers behind him also stopped in surprise.

For the end of the alley was blocked by a brown wall of monks. Brother Daniel, Brother Timothy, Brother James, and even Brother Paul. All the monks from the monastery had come to help their Pawtuxet brother!

The wall parted to let Squanto through. And then it closed again. The alley was a dead end. But Squanto jumped on a rain barrel and hoisted himself onto a roof. He saw the masts of the *Archangel* and its white sails rising in the nearby harbor.

"Stand aside, Friar!" Harding bellowed.

Soldiers with swords and muskets advanced. But the monks would not move. As the soldiers tried to pass, the Brothers stuck out their moccasined feet and tripped them. Even Brother Paul sent a soldier sprawling.

Squanto looked down and saw Maushop. He leaped through the air, hair flying behind him like the wings of a hawk. Squanto dropped onto the horse's back and galloped away.

There was no point trying to pass the stubborn monks. Harding led his men around the corner. "Keep looking! He mustn't . . ."

But the officer never finished his sentence. With a wild cry, Squanto and

Maushop hurtled toward them like a herd of buffalo! The soldiers scattered like bowling pins, clearing the warrior's path to the harbor.

In the distance, the *Archangel* swung close to the dock. Harding and his soldiers found horses of their own and resumed the chase.

Meanwhile, Sir George's fancy carriage had rolled to a stop. The merchant stamped furiously down the dock, shaking with rage at the report that his Squanto had escaped. Someone would pay for this!

But his angry thoughts were interrupted by a tremendous commotion. Sir George looked up and saw Squanto thundering straight toward him! Sir George drew a dainty engraved pistol from his sash and pointed it with shaking hands.

Squanto and Maushop leaped over Sir George and sailed through the air to land with a clatter on the deck of the *Archangel*. Wind filled her sails and the ship picked up speed!

Sir George waved his pistol and hopped up and down. "Stop that ship!" he shrieked. Sir George didn't see Harding and his soldiers until it was too late.

The soldiers' galloping horses skidded on the wet dock. Their riders struggled to stay in the saddle. Harding flew over his horse's head and slammed into Sir George. The two dropped into the water with a loud SPLASH!

Sir George kicked and sputtered. "Harding, you're fired!"

Aboard the ship, Captain Dermer made an important decision. He knew in his heart that it would be wrong to return Squanto to captivity. And so the *Archangel* sailed off toward the New World.

CHAPTER

10

▼△▼△▼△▼△▼

When Squanto could no longer see the monks waving from the shore, he turned and was happy to see Epenow on the deck of the ship. The warriors spent many weeks together as the *Archangel* crossed the Atlantic Ocean.

One night, while the English sailors slept in their swaying hammocks, the two warriors talked quietly.

"You have won the trust of the English," Squanto observed.

"The English are greedy," Epenow said. "I promised them gold."

"And where is this gold?" Squanto wondered.

Epenow smiled a wise smile. "I learned many things from the English. They taught me how to lie."

Lying was something unknown to the tribes of the New World. Squanto was not sure what to think of his friend now that Epenow had adopted this shameful practice. Could he be trusted?

"I learned from the English too," Squanto told his companion. "I found friends among them."

The sachem's eyes flared with anger. He said hotly, "Our friends are the people we are going home to, the Nausetts, the Pawtuxets. To my tribe I am loyal, and to my family and my son, Pequod, who will be a great warrior one day."

"I, too, am loyal to my tribe and family," said Squanto. "I have a bride, Nakooma, whose wedding gift I still keep with me." He touched the hawk feather in his hair. "New friends do not threaten my loyalty."

The older man spoke with disdain. "You are a fool. The white man is not your friend. He will only betray you."

Squanto was saddened to see his friend had become so bitter. Squanto knew that among the whites there were both good and bad, just as there were among the tribes of his homeland. He was glad he had been among such good men in the monastery. Epenow had seen only bad white men, like Sir George. This was not a true representation.

Many days passed. The ship survived storms; Squanto survived the bad food and boredom. His mind was always on home and the bride who waited for him there.

And then came the great day when a sailor cried, "Land ho!"

Squanto and Epenow looked upon the misty shores of their forest homeland. Waves splashed white foam over the dark rocks.

Captain Dermer searched the shore with a brass tube, a "spyglass" that brought things closer to the eye. "For us it's a new world, full of new promises and new beginnings," Dermer said.

"It's not new or old," Squanto replied. "It is our land."

Dermer smiled and offered the spyglass. "Do you recognize these shores?"

Squanto did not need the glass to know the place. Epenow spoke instead. "That is the home of my people."

Squanto nodded. "The Nausetts. I wish the Pawtuxets were there to celebrate our return."

"You will celebrate with Nakooma and your family soon enough," Epenow teased.

"Not for two more days," said Squanto. Now that he was so close to seeing his bride and family again, the waiting was agony! Squanto walked away from the other men so they would not see his emotion.

* * *

On the shore, Epenow's young son Pequod signaled his warriors with the mournful cry of the loon. They had seen the great canoe in the waters offshore. The Nausett women gathered the children and hurried for shelter. The white men might be invading. The people who had stolen their chief had returned!

A smaller canoe came out of the fog. It was paddled by many white men armed with muskets. Pequod raised his spear. Other warriors aimed their bows.

Then a voice came out of the mist. "*Moqo*, Pequod." His father's voice! "No, Pequod," it called.

The warriors were stunned to hear Epenow's voice. They had thought the sachem was dead. One by one they lowered their weapons.

That night the people danced and feasted around a roaring bonfire. They celebrated a miracle: their chief had returned! Epenow sat in a special place of honor, dressed in the sachem's finery. Sparks swirled up to the stars on a spiral of smoke. Wood popped and crackled. The white moon glowed over the dark, rolling sea where the *Archangel* lay anchored.

Dermer watched the ceremonies with great interest. His sailors drank rum and ridiculed the rituals. When Epenow cast his eyes on the Englishmen, his face grew hard and cold. But his face warmed with pride as Pequod led the young warriors in a game. They took turns shooting flaming arrows at a log floating in the sea. Pequod's arrow found its mark, and his chest swelled with a young man's triumph.

More sailors rowed the *Archangel*'s launch to shore, bringing food for the feast. Squanto was aboard the small boat, and swimming beside him was his horse.

The great beast reached the sandy shore and rose from the moonlit water. It shook droplets from its coat as it walked onto the beach.

Pequod and his friends gasped. "Maushop!" It was just as the ancient tales had told.

Squanto led Maushop to the young warrior and handed Pequod the horse's reins. Then he smiled and strolled to the bonfire.

Squanto sat next to Epenow and said, "When I see your son, I know I am no longer a boy."

"It is my hope he will follow me as sachem of the Nausett tribe," Epenow said. But he watched his reckless son with doubt in his heart. The boy had so much to learn, and his courage was not tempered with wisdom.

"He has a great teacher now that his father has returned," Squanto said.

Epenow was flattered, but worry nagged at his heart. Since the white men had landed on this shore, so much had changed. "Squanto, will you return to your home tomorrow?"

"I will leave at dawn," Squanto replied.

Epenow could feel his friend's eagerness, but he looked away into the orange flames. Epenow knew more than he could say. But before he could speak, Dermer addressed him. "My men and I will sleep tonight on our ship. We thank you for your hospitality. In the morning, we will trade with your people."

Epenow looked at the white man with a hunter's eyes. "Yes. In the morning there will be a trade."

* * *

Squanto woke before the sun had risen, restless to be on his way. The sooner he left, the sooner he would see Nakooma! Then, as sleep fell away from him, Squanto heard voices shouting. He crept from the wigwam. Stars still shone in the sky and the sun was just a glow over the water. It was too early for cooking fires, but he smelled smoke and sensed trouble.

And then Squanto saw flames dancing on the water. The *Archangel* was on fire!

Squanto ran to the beach, looking frantically for a canoe. He found one, but had to drag it to the water. While he did that, Squanto looked out and saw Epenow and his warriors paddling to the shore. Squanto hurried to put his canoe in the water, knowing that many sailors would drown if they did not get help soon.

The Nausetts' canoes ran aground, and Squanto saw that the men wore war paint and feathers. Their flesh was striped with red, black, white, and yellow paint. Red stood for blood; black for death; white for the spirit world; and yellow for the sun.

The Nausetts held spears and tomahawks, and their blood was hot from battle. A few warriors grabbed Squanto and pulled him back through the cold, shallow water to shore. Squanto struggled with them. Then Epenow's canoe glided to the beach.

"This is not our way!" Squanto shouted.

The sachem shouted back. His voice was hoarse. "No, it is their way, the way of the English!"

He stepped out of his canoe.

Squanto said, "You welcome them to your village, then slaughter them in their sleep."

Epenow replied, "They came to our land to trade and stole our best warriors."

Face to face with Squanto, the sachem pulled Dermer's hat from his belt and threw it in the dirt. The two men glared at each other.

"You have punished a good man for other men's cruelty," Squanto said angrily.

"I have killed!" Epenow shouted. "I am a warrior! You have forgotten who you are!"

"I have never forgotten!" Squanto lunged at Epenow and wrestled him to the ground. They fought, until Epenow's warriors grabbed Squanto and put spears against his chest.

Epenow stood and brushed sand from his leggings. "Go to your village, Squanto. See what the English have brought to your people. Then judge me for what I have done."

Squanto heard Maushop whinnying and young warriors cheering. Pequod rode up on the horse.

Squanto set out on foot carrying his meager possessions on his back. Epenow's words had turned the fever of his anticipation to cold dread. He did not know what he would find.

Yet he still hoped he would find his tribe celebrating the feast of the Green Corn, as they had for all the years of his life and long before his birth.

He soon came to the meadow where he had hunted deer with his father and kinsmen. The funnel trap was broken. The stakes had fallen. The sight of it deepened Squanto's dread, but he continued on.

He crossed the forest, which was filled with white birches like spirits of the dead. Squanto pushed branches aside and remembered how he and the warriors had returned to the village with their kill on the day before his wedding. Squanto stopped. He heard only the hollow hammering of a woodpecker on a nearby birch tree and a raven's harsh croak.

He left the shelter of the trees and looked down upon the Pawtuxet village. The wigwams were ripped and weathered. A red fox froze by the ruins of the long house. The hungry hunter stared at Squanto as if *he* were the intruder, then bounded away. The corn fields were choked with weeds. The canoes and fishing traps rotted on the beach. The village had the silence of the grave.

Squanto's heart shrank. The backpack slipped from his shoulders. His bow and arrows fell from numb fingers as he walked through the ruins. His feet took him to the wedding wigwam — only a shell of bent saplings and split birch.

Squanto fell to his knees and clutched the hawk feather to his chest. He could not contain his sorrow, and he wailed, "Nakooma!" His voice was carried up into the empty sky.

CHAPTER
11

▼▲▼▲▼▲▼

Squanto dragged all the belongings of the Pawtuxet people to the center of the village: deerskin clothing, birch baskets, snowshoes, cradle boards, tanning frames, canoes, traps, lacrosse sticks, arrows, axes, and hoes.

He built a great bonfire. The flames leaped up — a funeral pyre for his tribe. Squanto fed the hungry blaze with all he could find. He searched the sand and the grass and found one last thing, but he could not throw it on the fire. He lifted the wampung belt that belonged to his father. Squanto turned it over in his hands, lost in memory.

"The English. Their sickness brought death to your tribe," Epenow said.

Stunned with grief, Squanto barely saw the Nausett warrior beside him. They stood silent for a long time.

Finally, Squanto said, "My father wore this belt, as his father before him, and his before him. I was to wear it next. It was their strength and wisdom that this belt honored. Now I fear those things will be lost."

Epenow thought for a while. "Come back with me. You are welcome among the Nausetts."

"No. I belong here, with the memories of my people," Squanto said.

Epenow nodded. He watched as Squanto took a blackened stick from the fire and smeared streaks of soot on his cheeks and throat. Black was the color of death and eternal rest.

"I will wear their ashes and carry their spirit with me," said Squanto.

Epenow grabbed the young warrior's wrist. "The spirit is heavy with defeat." He gazed into Squanto's eyes and spoke sternly, like a father scolding for a child's good. "They will come again, the English. We both know this. When they do, you'll do your people honor by avenging their death. That is the wisdom you seek."

Squanto just stared at the man. Epenow

released his wrist and nodded farewell. He walked away without looking back.

Squanto watched him disappear into the forest. Epenow's words echoed in Squanto's mind long after the warrior was gone. He looked down at the wampung belt and lay it in the dirt before him. He sat cross-legged by the fire with his hands on his knees. Squanto stared at the flames. No hint of emotion crossed his blackened face.

The flames had died and night had fallen. Squanto still sat by the pile of smoking wood staring into nothingness, fighting to stay awake on his silent vigil. A tear escaped his eye and rolled down the soot on his cheek.

Dawn came and found him curled in the dirt, asleep. A hawk cried in the distance.

Squanto's eyes fluttered open. He looked up groggily and squinted to see the hawk vanish in the bright morning sun.

He rose and made a circle of stones. Squanto burned sweet grass and cleansed the air, sitting in the middle of the circle, finding harmony with nature.

* * *

Squanto built himself a lean-to with bent saplings and strips of birch bark, as his people had always built them. He had hunted and fished and was drying food before a small fire.

Squanto sensed something. He could not hear it or see it, but something was not right. He listened and heard a squirrel chattering. He listened more and heard the lonely cry of a loon. Perhaps he was wrong. Squanto lay a stone on the bark to anchor it to the lean-to frame. Then he picked up another piece of bark.

He finished his lean-to, but something still bothered Squanto. He went back to the ruined village, alert to danger. Squanto crouched low, slinking through the dense brush.

He stopped behind a bush and parted the branches. Through the green leaves, Squanto saw Englishmen standing in a circle around freshly dug graves. He recognized their dark clothing: Puritans.

* * *

The Puritans, who were also called Pilgrims, had anchored their ship, the *Mayflower*, in the bay. There they had set up a crude wooden sign that said "Plymouth."

Miles Standish had pounded the sign into the ground with a rock. His half-dozen soldiers patrolled the area with their muskets at the ready.

Squanto would have recognized some of the men, had he noticed them the day of the riot. William Bradford and Dr. Fuller were among the surviving members of the colonial party. Many of the Pilgrims had died from disease on their ship as they sailed to the New World.

They had nervously walked through the empty Pawtuxet village. Bradford worried that the Indians would return to their village. But Standish approved of the site — they were protected on all sides.

Standish assured them that if the inhabitants returned, they would be met with force. That's what he was paid for.

James Carver suggested they should bury their dead before they settled in. Bradford said, "Our brothers and sisters deserve a proper burial. This is someone else's home."

Nevertheless, they found a spot outside the village, and that is where Squanto discovered them. Dr. Fuller led the others in prayer over the heaped graves. Bradford held the hand of his five-year-old daughter while Fuller intoned, "We thank Thee, Lord, for answering our prayers and carrying us on our pilgrimage to this distant land. Gather into eternity the souls of our brothers and sisters whose lives were sacrificed to a higher and greater purpose. Amen."

The people prayed in silence with gentle sobs of grief. Squanto could understand their feelings. Yet when he saw the bearded man with the helmet and breastplate scanning the forest with a warrior's eye, hatred flamed in his heart.

Squanto reached for an arrow. Only one remained in the birch-bark quiver. He counted the soldiers and their muskets. This was a battle he couldn't win.

Then Squanto saw a soldier walk toward him. The man did not see him. Squanto slipped his arrow back into the quiver and carefully retreated.

* * *

Miles Standish, Bradford, Dr. Fuller, and James Carver stood in the old Pawtuxet long house. A fat candle dripped wax on a cargo chest. The settlers had stacked their provisions in the birch-bark building.

"The women and children will sleep in the three structures in the center of the village," Standish said. "The men will take the surrounding structures."

Dr. Fuller was concerned. "I fear these buildings will not withstand a severe winter. We must cut wood to build with before the weather changes."

"Indeed, shelter is one concern," Carver agreed. "But most of our food is either gone or spoiled. We have only a two-day supply left."

This was bad news: to have come so far and endured so much, only to be in danger of starvation. And they had been in the New World such a short time!

"I'll send out a patrol," Standish said. "Two soldiers to look for game and firewood."

This made the Pilgrims even more concerned. They knew they were surrounded by Indians. With two of Standish's men gone, there would be only four left to defend the Pilgrims should the Indians attack.

Bradford felt he needed to break the gloomy mood. "Faith is our most abundant surplus, brothers. Whoever lived here chose this place well. It will supply us with all we need to survive. The Lord will take care of the rest."

And so the soldiers were sent out into the endless forest. They clutched their muskets against the terrible fear of this alien world where even the plants were strange. Who knew what sort of animals lurked among the leaves, which were thicker than a London fog? And, of course, what about the wild savages of the woods who were said to be more vicious than any beast who walked on four legs?

The soldiers stepped cautiously through the ferns slapping at their boots. Their breastplates were heavy, and their thick boots crashed loudly through the underbrush.

Misty shafts of fog floated eerily between strange, white-trunked trees. The soldiers jumped in fear at a sudden, loud screech.

When the big, blue bird fluttered past, the men sighed with relief. One managed a smile. But when they started walking again, the other had the peculiar feeling that someone was following them.

When he turned to look, he saw nothing but green forest. The soldiers continued. Had he looked a little longer, he would have seen three Nausett warriors emerge like ghosts from the mist. Pequod was among them. They were painted and ready for battle.

The soldier turned again and saw only forest. He relaxed. His mind was playing tricks on him.

And then an arrow pierced him between his shoulder blades. His finger twitched and his musket fired as the soldier flopped to the ground, dead.

His companion spun around in panic. He saw the three warriors sprinting toward him with stone axes. With their paint and tattoos, they looked barcly human to the soldier.

He aimed and fired. The musket boomed in the forest. Birds shrieked. And a cloud of gun smoke drifted up.

The soldier missed, but the warriors dove for cover, unsure of the power of his weapon. The soldier bolted for a thicket of trees. Pequod stood and aimed and put an arrow in the white man's arm.

Later, Pequod was filled with the glory of his deeds as he rode Maushop along the shore to his father's camp. He leaped off the horse before it stopped. He told his father the tale of his great battle.

The other warriors were infected with Pequod's excitement. Epenow embraced his son, the hero.

* * *

Squanto had made many arrows. He stared blankly into space as he sharpened his tomahawk. When that task was done, he reached into a small wooden bowl and dipped his fingers into red, muddy paint. War paint. Red, like blood. Squanto smeared it on his face. But he stopped. He looked down and his gaze fell upon the wampung belt beside the fire.

It was as if two warriors argued in his heart: his father and Epenow. Squanto thought of the tales of the wampung belt, and the tales he hoped to add to it. He thought of the dead village and Brother Daniel. He thought for a long time.

At dusk, Squanto slinked along the edge of the forest. His quiver was full. His spear was in his hand. The sun had left a red stripe like a bleeding wound where the sky met the land.

He looked down on the Pawtuxet village, the Pilgrim's village now. Squanto saw the Englishmen in their black clothes unloading crates and building a wooden barricade.

Then he saw a wounded soldier stumble into the arms of his comrades. People ran to his aid and carried the man into the long house. While they were busy, Squanto slipped between wigwams and drying racks. He hid outside the door to the long house.

"Get me some clean muslin and boil me some water," a man said.

A soldier ran out. He brushed past Squanto, hiding in the shadows.

Inside, the wounded soldier lay unconscious. The arrow in his arm had broken off. The bloody tip protruded from his sleeve. His face was white.

Dr. Fuller rolled up his sleeves. Standish

looked at the wound and fixed the others with a steely look. "Indians."

Horror swept across the faces of the Pilgrim leaders like early frost on a spring field.

"Every available man will take up a musket," Standish declared. "When they come, we'll aim to kill."

"No! We mustn't fight back!" Bradford protested. "That is against everything we believe. Perhaps this was only meant to warn."

"A warning? These are savages," Standish said.

Carver agreed. "Mr. Standish is right. We've lived too long under persecution and fear. I say we fight for what must be ours."

Bradford pleaded with them. "It is certain we are sorely outnumbered. Surely we don't intend to kill them all."

Standish frowned with grim determination. "If we must, Mr. Bradford. If we must." He turned to Carver. "Tell the men to unload the arsenal."

Carver nodded and went out the door.

Squanto slipped off into the night. He didn't see Standish leave, or the worried look in Bradford's eyes.

* * *

When the morning mist rose off the forest floor, Epenow led two dozen warriors running at a steady pace, weaving through the trees, silent as deer. The only sound was the muted drumming of Maushop's hooves as Pequod brought up the rear.

When they reached the Pawtuxet village where the white men cowered like deer in a trap, the warriors fanned out behind trees and bushes. To the white men's feeble eyes, the warriors would be invisible.

The Pilgrims didn't hear the Nausetts coming. But they knew the warriors would. The men crouched behind the barricade, holding the heavy, oily muskets fresh from their crates.

Standish was ready. His armor gleamed. His jaunty plumes ruffled in the morning breeze. His eyes were cold and ready for battle.

Bradford was the only man without a gun. His eyes were troubled.

Epenow saw his warriors were in place, ready for his signal. He started to raise his spear, but stopped. A small, knowing smile curled his lips. He saw Squanto crossing the meadow between the forest and the village: Squanto, in war paint, hidden from the Pilgrims by the tall grass. He was holding a quiver full of arrows, a spear, and with a razor-sharp tomahawk tucked in his wampung belt.

Squanto crossed the tall grasses where he and his bride had first seen the big, black ship. He slinked closer to the village, taking cover behind a tree. He turned and looked back at Epenow. The Nausett were not invisible to Squanto.

Their eyes met. The older warrior smiled to his brother in arms. He motioned with his spear for Squanto to take the honor of first blood.

Standish knew in his bones the battle must soon begin. He scanned the trees for a sign of the enemy. This kind of war was new to him. In England and on the continent of Europe, soldiers lined up against each other on open battlefields. Only thieves struck from cowardly ambush. These savages knew nothing of the art of war, but that did not make them any less dangerous.

Epenow watched Squanto, waiting for him to finally act like a warrior and avenge his people. Hiding in the tall grass, Squanto crept closer to the white men.

The young warrior paused. He saw the Nausett poised to attack. The Pilgrims held their shiny muskets, ready to kill and die. Tension and hatred were everywhere. Squanto thought of Epenow's hatred and Sir

George's greed. He remembered Dermer's kindness and the courage of Brother Daniel. Then he heard his father's words and Nakooma's gentle voice. It was more than his heart could bear.

The time to act was now! Squanto stepped out from his hiding place. Tall and proud, he walked fearlessly toward the log barricade.

"Squanto! What are you doing?" Epenow cried out.

"What has to be done. What my father would have done." Squanto did not look back.

Standish saw the lone Indian approaching. The warrior bristled with weapons. His face and bare chest were streaked with bright war paint.

"There they are!" Standish cried. "Ready!"

Squanto drew his tomahawk and threw it on the ground.

"Aim!"

Squanto dropped his bow and quiver of arrows.

Epenow motioned for his warriors to move in, fearing Squanto would need their help. The warriors stepped into the clearing twenty yards behind the Pawtuxet.

Squanto cracked his spear over his knee and tossed the pieces away. He continued his steady walk to the barricade.

"Shoot him!" Carver shouted furiously.

Dr. Fuller objected. "But, Sir, he's unarmed."

Standish didn't know what to do. The warrior's actions were a complete mystery to him.

"Shoot him," Carver repeated.

Bradford stood up. "No, wait. He means no harm."

Squanto stopped ten yards from the gleaming muzzles of the muskets and looked death in the face. "Enough."

The Pilgrims' jaws dropped. The warrior spoke English! They couldn't have been more surprised if a cow had spoken.

Standish aimed his musket. "It's a trick!"

"Too much blood!" Squanto cried.

Suddenly all was still.

"Too much blood on this land," said Squanto. "Too many tears. All of my people are gone. More of your people will die. Put down your weapons, all of you."

Epenow could not believe his ears. The son of Mooshawset had gone mad with grief! The sachem did not know what to do. His battle plan had been ruined. His men were exposed and the enemy alerted.

Pequod was furious. He had come to fight. He wanted glory!

The boy charged straight at the white

men, shooting arrows as he ran. His war cry echoed in his own ears, terrible as thunder!

And there was thunder, as Standish's musket boomed and Pequod dropped with a bullet in him.

Epenow was thunderstruck. His son had fallen! All his warriors looked to their sachem for the signal to retaliate. Instead, to their shock, Epenow rushed to Pequod and cradled his wounded son.

Squanto stood protectively over the Nausett father and son. Epenow looked up at his friend, eyes filled with confusion and anger.

Squanto looked from the anguished father to the angry warriors and then back to the Pilgrims poised to kill. He sank to his knees with tears in his eyes.

"Now kill me! Kill me!" he cried to the Pilgrims. "And they will kill you."

He pointed to Pequod. "And more of us will die. And we will kill each other until there's nothing left but ashes and bones. Nothing but children who will never be born."

Squanto looked at Epenow. "Is that what we fight for?"

There was no answer. Squanto said, "Enough. Enough killing. Not one more. We must end it here and now."

Where there had almost been war, now there was only silence. Squanto's words rang in everyone's ears.

Dr. Fuller said, "I can help." He knelt beside Pequod. "We need to stop the bleeding. Take him inside."

Two soldiers reached for the boy. Epenow grabbed Dr. Fuller's shoulder, but Squanto restrained the sachem.

Epenow said, "If he dies, we will kill them all."

His warriors struggled to restrain their fury. They had come for a fight, and there was none. The Pilgrims wondered how long this peculiar peace would last.

Squanto and Epenow followed the wounded boy into the long house. They watched the white medicine man work with his sharp, shiny tools, boiling water and cloth.

Day passed into night. The English soldiers and Nausett warriors warily watched each other across a crackling fire. Both sides still clutched their weapons.

Some of the Nausett chanted a prayer for Pequod. And as they chanted, the Pilgrims began to pray. Algonquin and English mixed in a rhythmic harmony pleasing to all ears.

At last, Dr. Fuller held up the bullet. "The bullet is out, but the wound is not clean. I'm afraid fever may set in."

Epenow's eyes flickered with panic. Squanto knelt and opened his pouch. He took out herbs and crushed them in a bowl of water.

"How is he now?" Bradford asked anxiously.

"It is in the hands of Kissuulk," Squanto said. "We must wait."

And they waited together through the long night. When dawn came, Epenow knelt by his son, watching his face for any sign of life. At last, Pequod's eyes opened. He would be well again.

Exhausted, Epenow stepped from the long house. His face showed no expression. His warriors and the Pilgrims looked to him. Epenow stepped aside and Pequod shuffled out. He was no longer a wild warrior, but a wounded boy.

"My son has been given his life. We will leave this village now," Epenow said.

The warriors lowered their weapons. Reluctantly, Standish and his men lay down their muskets.

Squanto put out his hand. "Goodbye, Epenow."

Epenow took the Pawtuxet's hand. "Goodbye, Squanto," he said formally. And then his voice warmed. "Thank you, my friend."

In the peace that followed, and with Squanto's help, the Pilgrims planted their first crops. Squanto placed four kernels of corn in the rich soil: one for each of the four winds, and a fish head to feed the growing seeds. Squanto showed them how to tap the maple trees for their sweet sap, and how to dig clams, trap eels, and weave grass nets to catch small fish. They planted pumpkins, squash, and beans.

He showed the children how to chase the hungry birds from the fields. The men learned how to build traps, and make bows and arrows so they could hunt deer, moose, bears, ducks, and the big, gobbling turkeys that ran wild in the woods.

In the summer, beautiful stalks of corn stood tall against the blue sky. Just as the tender plants thrived in this New World, so did the children of the Pilgrims. They played with Squanto, and he taught them the ways of the forest.

And in the fall when the leaves turned as gold as Sir George's ring and as orange as flames, people from all around what had been the Pawtuxet village came for a great harvest feast.

They all sat together at long tables, like

the monks of Squanto's "tribe" across the sea. They all bowed their heads as Dr. Fuller spoke. "Heavenly Father, we thank Thee for this bountiful harvest and for bringing so many of us together on this joyous day. We humbly ask Thee for Thy blessing. Amen."

And then they feasted: Epenow and Bradford, Standish and Squanto. For there was much to be thankful for: the roast turkeys and ducks, the sweet corn and nuts, and bright red cranberries sweetened with maple syrup.

Then Squanto stood and raised a glass. The people were quiet. For the Pawtuxet was a great man to them all.

Squanto said, "In the world there are many people with many customs, speaking many languages. But there is only one moon, only one sun, only one tribe."

The people rejoiced, and went back to their feasting. But then Squanto heard something. He looked up at the sky and saw a hawk. He followed the bird to the water.

When he came to the ocean, Squanto saw canoes. *People arriving late to the feast*, he thought.

The first canoe beached, and two warriors climbed out. And Squanto knew them! A shock ran through his body. Squanto raced to the men: his old friends, Pocknet and Attaquin!

"Squanto? Are you . . . a ghost?" Pocknet asked in a voice as shy as Brother James's.

"I don't understand," Squanto stammered as he hugged his long-lost friends. "Where have you — ?"

Pocket said, "Some of us survived the sickness. We have been living with the Narragansetts."

Squanto's spirit soared with hope. He could barely say, "Nakooma?"

The faces of his friends revealed nothing. Squanto's heart sank.

Then Attaquin smiled as a woman's voice exclaimed, "Squanto!"

Nakooma stood in a canoe, too excited to care that the vessel almost overturned. It didn't matter, because Squanto was already splashing through the shallow water to his bride.

Nakooma leaped into the warm waters of the sea. The beautiful braids of her wedding day bounced around her shoulders as she rushed into Squanto's arms. The hawk circled overhead.

It would be a new beginning for them all.